Dylan and the
Deadly Dimension

Mark Bardwell

Published in the UK by Everything with Words Limited
3rd Floor, Premier House
12-13 Hatton Garden, London EC1N 8AN
www.everythingwithwords.com

A CIP catalogue record for this book is available for the British Library
ISBN 978-1-911427-03-2

Printed and bound in Great Britain by Clays Ltd, St Ives plc.

For Joe

1

IT WAS THE morning Dylan saw a snake in the bathroom sink that things became strange. It was two weeks to his twelfth birthday. He had just been brushing his teeth. As he rinsed the basin, he noticed something odd beneath the plughole. Just below the grating, he could make out something made of black, red and yellow stripes. Peering closer, leaning in as close as he could get, he saw glistening scales coiled round in tight rings. Looked like a snake. How would *a snake* have managed to get into the u-bend? Dylan strained for a closer look when—all of a sudden—the coils moved and the snake's head darted upwards. He jumped back in fright. He crept back towards the sink and peered in again. There was nothing there. It was just an ordinary plughole.

'Dylan, get a move on.' His dad's voice called from downstairs. 'You've got thirty seconds, or I'm going to leave without you.'

Dylan and his dad, Jim, had just moved back to Croydon, the town where Dylan had been born and raised until the age of seven. The past few years they had been continually on the move, up and down the country, changing houses like shoes because of Jim's job as an environmental scientist that required him to work here, there and everywhere. Dylan's mum had died in a car accident when he was six years old.

Dylan didn't like Croydon. It was overcrowded and smelly and reminded him of his mum's absence. It was the summer holidays. Not having started his new school, Dylan didn't have any friends in the town. That suited him fine. He was tired of having to make new friends every time they moved. There didn't seem to be much point in trying—the chances were that they would just end up somewhere else, yet again. Although his dad had said they would be settling permanently this time.

They were heading into town. His dad needed to get some bits and bobs from the shops, while Dylan was eager to get to the library. He was an avid reader—he almost always had his nose in a book. Books were consistent and loyal. Wherever he went, he could take them with him. And they stayed with him long after he finished them, roaming around inside his head. He felt so strongly connected with some characters in stories that they felt more like his friends than anyone in real life. They seemed to have stepped out of the books, out of their stories. He could feel their presence in the dull house where he lived and in the flat swirl of the everyday with its insistent detail, the do this and do that. They came with him into that empty no go country of his mum's absence.

As the car had been playing up in the week, they got the bus into town. Dylan's dad was keen on public transport. 'Better for the environment,' he said. They got off the bus opposite the library and arranged to meet up again in a shopping centre an hour later. It was the middle of a busy Saturday morning. People were darting this way and that, bumping into each other and rushing around as if they were buying supplies for the end of the world. Dylan dodged between them and made his way down the steps that led into the library.

He felt at home inside libraries. The books lined the shelves like hundreds of different worlds sitting next to each other. Worlds that didn't exist until he read the words contained in their pages. It excited him not knowing which of these worlds he would be visiting next. He spent half an hour reading the backs of books and glancing inside their pages. Before long he had a carefully selected pile of books to take out. The lady at the counter smiled at him. Although they had only been back in Croydon a few weeks, he had been to the library so often that the staff had started to recognise him.

There was some time to kill before meeting his dad, so he didn't rush. He sat on a bench for a little while reading one of his books. It was about a seagull, written from the seagull's perspective. It was odd, but he was enjoying it. He read the first chapter before deciding it was time to go. It was hot and sunny. Sitting in the heat had made Dylan feel a little dozy. He decided to make his way to the high street via a small covered parade of shops called St George's Walk that would provide some shade. It was more run down than the big shopping centres further down the high street. The shops and cafes were mainly independent, the sort that often spring up overnight and vanish just as quickly.

Walking down the parade, he saw a shop that he didn't remember from before. It was a tiny bookshop. Books were piled up in the window in unstable looking stacks. What could be seen of the shops interior, past the piles, was dimly lit and gave little away. A small sign above the window read 'Ebenezer Books - Second-Hand and Rare'. Despite a notice on the shop door saying 'Open', it looked very much closed, and not particularly inviting. But Dylan, being rather intrigued, walked up and tried the handle. It *was* open. He pushed the door slowly and went in. It was hard to make much out in the gloom. There were tall piles of books everywhere, creating a maze of passages. He couldn't see anyone behind the counter, but there must have been someone there because there was a dusty record player playing old sounding jazz music. Dylan wandered around the shop, almost tripping over the books. He still couldn't see anyone. There was a weird musty smell. He picked up some of the books. They all had strange titles, like *Transmutation in the Dance of Paraclemetides*, *Shrogwallops of Canterbury* or *Farming Backwards*. He wanted to spend some more time in there, but looking at his watch he saw that he only had five minutes before he was meant to be meeting his dad. He was walking past the counter towards the exit, when a reedy voice piped up out of nowhere.

'Who's that? Wait there!'

The voice had come from behind the vacant counter. Dylan froze and waited in confusion. A wavy bush of grey hair popped up and then rose slowly to reveal an old man attached to it. He must have been on the floor. He looked like he might have been napping, but there was an alert and possibly hostile look in his eyes. He was wiry thin and wore an old, but well kept, tweed suit and round glasses, which he was readjusting. He had a grey well-trimmed beard that contrasted with his wild mess of shaggy side-parted hair. There was something not quite right about him.

'Well then, what do we have here?' he said in his slightly high-pitched voice, leaning forward over the counter and peering through his glasses at Dylan. 'A young gentleman, eh?' he said, standing up straight. 'Well, what is it that you're after?'

'Oh, I was just browsing,' Dylan said nervously. The old man's stare was unnerving.

'Are you sure?' His thick white eyebrows arched questioningly. 'People never come here to browse. People only ever come to my shop if they're after something in particular. So what is it that you're after, my good sir?'

'Umm. I'm not... I'm not really sure.'

'Not really sure, you say? How can you not be sure, if you've come to my shop for something in particular?'

'Well, sorry, sir. I didn't mean I wasn't sure. I meant that I hadn't come here for anything in particular. I was just passing, you see, and the shop looked interesting, so I came in to look around.'

'Hmmm.' The old man folded his arms across his chest and stroked his beard. 'Most peculiar, most peculiar. And most unlikely. As I said, no one ever comes in here *just to browse*.' He eyed Dylan suspiciously. 'Are you sure that there's not something you came in here for? Maybe, *Trains That Never Went Anywhere*?' He held up a book that had been on the counter.

Dylan shook his head.

'Not much of a talker are we? Oh well. My name is Mr Ebenezer, as I'm sure you can work out from the shop name. And you are?'

'D-Dylan. Dylan Thompson,' Dylan stammered nervously. Mr Ebenezer was making him feel uncomfortable.

'Well, Master Thompson, I'm sure I will be seeing you soon enough, when you have remembered what it is you came to my shop for. Now if you don't mind, I'm rather busy.'

'Yes, of course,' said Dylan. 'Goodbye, Mr Ebenezer.'

'Yes, yes. Goodbye Master Thompson,' said Mr Ebenezer impatiently, his eyes focused on some papers he was fussing over on his counter.

Dylan crept out of the shop feeling rather confused. As he closed the door behind him, he could just hear the old man muttering. He couldn't make out enough to understand what he was talking about, but he felt a shudder run up and down his spine.

Strange things kept on happening. Each time, just before something happened, he would have this pins and needles sensation and a feeling that something wasn't right, something that he couldn't put his finger on. The following Monday, he was walking across the local playing fields. The sky was clear and blue and the sun was so bright it hurt to look up for more than a couple of seconds. He was halfway across when a tingling sensation ran down his spine. As this happened, he looked up and saw what he could only describe as a humongous dragonfly, two metres long and as thick as a log, carrying the figure of man silhouetted against the sky. The light was so sharp he closed his eyes. When he was able to look up again, there was nothing there.

A few days later he was on a train with his dad, on their way to visit his grandma. His dad was reading a newspaper while Dylan looked out of the window. The carriage was almost full. He was daydreaming amidst the background chatter when the pins and needles sensation ran down his spine once again, making him immediately alert. Standing in the middle of a passing field were two figures, arm in arm. Not too unusual in itself, but a closer look gave him a shock: one was a towering grizzly bear, and the respectably dressed man it linked arms with had the head of a badger and was smoking a pipe. Dylan was bewildered. He looked again to make sure, but the train had picked up speed and all was now a blur. He looked around the carriage. To his disbelief, no one seemed to have noticed anything out of the ordinary—there were no pressed noses against the windows or wild discussion about what people had just seen. Everyone carried on as normal. People were happily chatting to one another, reading or talking on their mobiles. His father was just sitting there with his paper, as if nothing had happened.

Something even more unnerving occurred a few days later. He was walking down the road close to his house. He wasn't looking at anything in particular when something caught his eye. In the slot of the post box across the road were two eyes peering out at him. Although he couldn't see the rest of the face, he could clearly see who it was. It was Mr Ebenezer from the bookshop. There was an unchanging look of disgust in his gaze, his bushy eyebrows pointing in a low, menacing swoop. It chilled Dylan. He closed his eyes and breathed deeply, hoping that when he looked again Mr Ebenezer's face would be gone. He opened his eyes to find Mr Ebenezer was still staring back, cold and unwavering. Dylan didn't know what to do, but he couldn't stay there. So he ran, and kept running for some time.

Dylan finally stopped in an underpass. He leant forward, hands on knees, ferociously out of breath. He gasped as his nostrils took in the smell of urine and litter that filled the dingy, grey tunnel. His lungs hurt. He couldn't understand what he had seen. It was ridiculous. Why had Mr Ebenezer been in the post-box? How did Mr Ebenezer get *inside* the post-box? Why was he staring at Dylan like that? That look... Dylan shuddered thinking about it. It made him feel a horrible lump deep in his belly. And then there were the other strange things that had been happening. Had other people been seeing these things?

Suddenly, Dylan became conscious of a shadow falling over him. Looking up, his eyes met those of a boy of a similar same age to himself. The eyes were narrowed, the head bent, as if the boy were trying get the weight of him. It was a spiteful kind of face. The boy was very thin, but a wiry kind of thin, like a spring pressed down and ready to poing off at any second. They looked at each other for a couple of moments before the boy spoke.

'Worr've we got here, eh, lads?' He said, still staring at Dylan. His voice sounded prematurely wounded by smoke.

Beside the boy who had spoken were three more. They were passing a cigarette between them and smirking knowingly at Dylan. One of them was a bulky, burly kind of lad, while the other two were rather average looking lunks. They didn't respond to the wiry boy's comment, just continued to smirk and drag on the cigarette.

'Well?' he said, squaring up to Dylan a little, 'Who are yer?'

Dylan stood up, but didn't say anything. The boy leant his face in a little.

'Wot you doin', down in Pete's Place? Wot you runnin' from? I saw yer. Like a hamster pooin' yerself.'

The other boys chuckled at this, as if the wiry boy, who must be Pete, had made a terribly witty remark.

Dylan still didn't speak. His heart started beating faster again, but he tried not to show it.

'Don't like talkin'?' Pete started walking round Dylan in a circle. The other boys closed in around him.

'Well—seeming as yer 'ere, fancy a smoke?' he said. The other boys chuckled again. Dylan stood his ground and hoped they would get bored.

Pete took the cigarette, nearly down to the stub, from

the burly boy. He leaned in towards Dylan again, uncomfortably close and grabbed his t-shirt tightly near the collar.

'Well, 'ere have some.'

The lit end of the cigarette came closer and closer to Dylan's face, when suddenly, as he could feel the heat of the glowing tip about to touch his skin, he pushed Pete back with all his strength.

'No,' he shouted.

But, Pete still had a firm grip on Dylan's t-shirt. They both went tumbling to the ground. Before he knew it, all four boys were round him, kicking and punching without a chance for him to get up. Suddenly they stopped. The burley boy was sitting on Dylan's chest so he couldn't get up and he felt too sore to put up much of a struggle. Pete bent down and pulled Dylan's wallet from his jeans.

'Give that back,' he said, reaching out for it, but the boy sitting on him shoved him back down. There wasn't much in it. Only a couple of pound coins. There was one other thing in there though.

'A *library* card?' said Pete as he pulled it out. 'Urr, looks like we've got some kind of little boffin here lads. Worr's his name? Dylan? What kind of stupid name is that? You know what we do wiv boffins, *Dylan*?'

'Hur, hur,' came the other boys' response.

Pete moved so his head was right above Dylan's. He

made a theatrical coughing noise, as if he was hacking up phlegm, and started building a dribble of spit from his pursed lips that threatened to drop onto Dylan's face at any second.

Dylan closed his eyes. As he did so, a voice came from the other side of the underpass.

'Oi! Leave the boy alone!' It was an adult's voice.

Suddenly Pete and his gang lost their confidence and sprinted out of there.

The man helped Dylan up. He asked if he was all OK, and if he should help him get home. Dylan thanked him, but shook his head and said he would be OK on his own.

He limped home feeling miserable, constantly looking over his shoulder in case Pete and those other boys came back for him. Everything was going wrong. He hated being back in Croydon. It felt like the whole place didn't want him there. He knew he could get another library card, but it still upset him nonetheless. He hoped he never saw those boys again.

2

IN THE DAYS after the incident with Pete and the other boys, he barely left his room and spent most of his time sitting cross legged on his bed with his nose in a book. He had lost interest in what was happening in the real world. The weather became temperamental. On a couple of days there were thunder storms. They almost cheered him up. He loved storms, if he was all dry at home and reading, listening to the rain thumping on the roof and window, thunder murmuring and bellowing in the background.

Dylan's dad was concerned. Every now and then he would turn up and lean in the door frame of Dylan's bedroom for a few minutes. He'd ask Dylan if he wanted to accompany him on his errands, or see if there were any activity groups he could join for the remainder of the holidays. He would stand in the door, a kind and helpless look on his face that made things worse. Dylan ignored him, his mind drifting into imaginary conversations with people from stories.

'I'm sorry.' He was looking at Dylan, trying to put so

much into the little he said. 'Maybe you need some friends.'

He wasn't a talker. He had moved in a sad silence after Dylan's mum had died. Dylan had escaped into books.

'I'm sorry,' repeated his dad, standing there, his lean figure in the door way, his face full of thoughts he didn't know what to do with.

Dylan looked up from his book. 'What for?' he said after a few seconds.

Jim looked out of the window. 'I don't know.' He scratched his chin. 'Dragging you around. Pulling you out of schools, making you move away from your friends. Not giving you the time you deserve.'

'I'm fine Dad, really,' Dylan said earnestly.

There was a pause for a few moments.

'You're not though, really, are you, Dylan? You've not been yourself at all recently. Not since we've come back to Croydon.'

Dylan barely left the house until the day of his birthday. He hadn't been expecting anything. His dad had said something about taking him to dinner in the evening, but that was about it.

However, he was woken up by blinding sunlight early in the morning when Jim pulled open the curtains without warning.

'Wake up, birthday boy!' he cried. 'I want you up and dressed—you're going on a birthday adventure!'

After a quick breakfast they set off. From East Croydon they took a train into London. Sitting on the train and looking out at the Thames before they arrived at Victoria, he felt a mixture of peace and excitement he hadn't felt for a long while. He kept looking round but everything was ordinary. No snakes lurking anywhere, no strange creatures flying through the air.

From Victoria they travelled to South Kensington where they spent a couple of hours visiting the Science Museum and the Natural History Museum. Dylan had been to them before, but they seemed like distant memories. He particularly enjoyed the dinosaurs in the Natural History Museum, and the bug section. The oldness of the building made it all the better too. It felt reassuring, and a lot more solid than modern buildings.

After lunch, they moved on to Covent Garden, visiting some of the stalls and watching the various street entertainers. There were all sorts including jugglers, mimes and comedians. It was busy and crowded.

They stopped to watch a magician attempting to saw a volunteer from the audience in half and pretending to get it wrong. Just when the performance was about to reach its climax, a shadow suddenly covered the whole square. Everyone in the crowd looked up in astonishment. Where there had been nothing but blue moments before, the whole sky was covered in dark clouds. It was impossible—no cloud could move that fast. A ferocious rain started pouring down. People were running and dashing for cover. Dylan could feel that tingling sensation moving down his spine, but this time it was a thousand times stronger. Some unseen force had rooted him to the spot.

After a few minutes, just as suddenly, the force let go. Rubbing his back, he looked around and noticed something very strange. Something very strange indeed. Everything had stopped. *Everything.* People were frozen in the position they were in just as the rain had started, running for cover. The rain was frozen in the air, birds were static in the sky, flags had stopped mid wave. Dylan looked at his father next to him. He had stopped too. He was staring blankly at the magician who looked very silly frozen in the middle of a dramatic pose, one eyebrow raised and a hand high in the air. It was eerie. As if Madame Tussauds had replaced everyone in Covent Garden with wax dummies. Dylan reached over to his dad and tugged on his sleeve. He didn't move at all. He was rock solid. It was the same with the rain—as if the air was filled with thousands of tiny bits of plastic instead of water. He took a couple of steps forward. The plastic rain was simply pushed out of the way.

He stood there for a couple of minutes, mesmerized by the awesome sight—a stillness full of something about to happen, something evil. Everyone frozen as statues, people and animals—a couple of pigeons in the air, a dog in mid bark, an angry woman, her face all screwed up into a shout, a sinister clown surrounded by children.

He felt someone bump into him from behind. Startled, he spun round. The person was in a long beige rain coat and had a bowler hat pulled low on his head so he couldn't see his face.

'Oh, sorry,' said the figure.

'Um, that's fine,' said Dylan, kind of relieved that there was someone else who hadn't been frozen.

'Well, who do we have here who's managed to escape being *stuckered*?' The figure lifted its head pushing its hat back.

Dylan took a couple of steps backwards in fright. It wasn't human. From the voice, he had expected to see the head of a youngish man, but there wasn't a face at all. Just a smooth, bone coloured oval shape, like an ostrich egg perched on a neck at a slant. The hand that had pushed the hat back consisted of three long stick thin fingers of similar white shell-like substance.

'Well, that's just charming,' the thing said. 'I'm not that ugly, am I?'

Dylan didn't know what to say and stood there on edge, wondering how it spoke without moving its lips... without *having* any lips.

The thing moved its head around, as if taking the place in.

'Hmmm...' It said. 'I'm getting fed up of being pulled this way and that. Where am I now?'

It took Dylan a moment to realise that the question was directed at him.

'Umm... London...' he ventured.

'London, hmm? Lon-don. I've not heard of a London before. Where's London?' It said, scratching its head with a three-fingered hand.

'Well. In England,' said Dylan. 'Er - on Earth.'

'Ah, that's more like it! Earth. I know where Earth is. But I haven't seen it looking like this. What I really would like to know, if you don't mind, is which reality are we in?'

'Reality?'

'Yes, yes. Are you quite alright? How ever could you forget which reality you're in? If you can't think of the name, do you at least know the co-ordinates?'

'No. Sorry. I'm afraid, I'm slightly confused.'

'You don't say?' The figure's tone was becoming impatient.

'Um...Sorry if this sounds rude. But what are you? And what's going on?'

'What *am* I? Well, I never!' The figure suddenly stood straight. 'Have I really? This must be one of them. This is an untapped reality! We could never be sure if it could be true—that there were closed realities. Young sir, are you saying that people here are unable to travel outside of this reality?'

'Well,' Dylan said slowly. 'I'm not sure what you mean exactly.'

'Then it must be! Whoever would have thought? And how, *on Kshar*, could I have got here, if it's closed?' He seemed quite excited. The figure looked around again.

'What's your name?' it asked.

'Dylan.'

'Well, Dylan. I'm delighted to make your acquaintance. My name is Rollovkarghjicznilegogh-Vylpophyngh.'

'Rollo...?'

'Rollovkarghjicznilegogh-Vylpophyngh.'

'Rollo-vik-arf-jics... Could I call you Rollo? I'm afraid I can't quite manage the rest.'

'I guess so, I guess so. Everyone else does. Anyway— you know what it means when things are stuckered? Trouble is what it means. We'd better look for somewhere safe to hide out until it's over.'

'Sorry, but what do you mean by *stuckered*? What sort of trouble?' asked Dylan.

Just then there was a loud and horrible noise, as if two gigantic metal gears were grinding together.

'No time to explain,' said Rollo grabbing Dylan's arm and pulling him towards a nearby shop. Dylan tried to resist, reaching towards his dad, but Rollo's grip was too strong. The hand that gripped him was like bone, but had more weight and had a smoother, glossy feel to it.

He pulled Dylan into a glass-fronted shop that sold gadgets and gifts.

'Not the best hiding place,' he said. 'But we've not much choice.'

They hid behind the counter and peered out into the square. The grinding noise was becoming even louder. Dylan put his hands over his ears in pain. Suddenly, what looked like a boiling cloud of some black substance appeared about twenty foot from the ground. The cloud was ripped open and a monstrous thing came falling out making a weird, strangled roaring sound. It was big, grey, and about the size of a baby elephant. Some kind of gloop kept dripping from its glistening body. It had four legs, two arms and raised ridges along its back. The face had two large human-like eyes and a wide mouth filled with numerous drooling, pointed teeth. It careened frantically around the square knocking people this way and that, continuing to roar all the while. Dylan stood there rooted in fear. He couldn't take his eyes off... whatever it was.

Three more creatures dropped out of the black cloud. They looked like very stocky men, of around seven feet high. They wore dark suits that looked like police uniforms, and helmets which covered their heads as far as the nose. Their big jaws really jutted out of their face. Long, rhino-like horns came out of their chins. They carried staffs that had whips attached to the end. They didn't look friendly. Rollo put a restraining hand on Dylan.

All three of the horned creatures went straight towards the rampaging beast. Expertly they surrounded it and struck it with their whips. The beast cowered to a standstill. Again and again the horned men whipped the creature, coiling their whips tightly around its arms. With much effort, they began to drag the beast, now in too much pain to struggle, below the dark cloud. They were shouting something in strange deep voices, heaving and pulling the beast off the ground with their staffs. With a roar, the beast disappeared into a great hole in the black cloud, pulling the horned men in with it. Instantly, the hole began to close.

Shocked, Dylan looked at Rollo for an explanation, but Rollo was already making for the door.

'I'd better get out of here,' he said, 'Or I never will. I'd say until we meet again, Dylan, but I very much doubt that we will.'

He ran from the door towards the hole, which had shrunk to almost nothing. Dylan ran out after him.

'Wait!' he called.

Rollo continued to run. As he neared the hole, he pulled a kind of rope from a pocket, flinging one end into it. In an instant, just as it was closing, Rollo was sucked into the hole.

Before Dylan had a chance to think, the rain started pummelling down again all around him. He looked around. Everyone was back on their feet, as they were, completely unharmed and unaware that anything had happened, still dashing for cover. He stood there unable to understand.

'Dylan,' his dad's voice called, as if nothing strange had happened at all. 'Come on, let's get under some shelter.'

3

D YLAN LOOKED AT himself in his bedroom mirror as he tied his school tie. A brand new uniform for a brand new school. It was like looking at a stranger.

He wasn't nervous about starting a new school. This was his 5th or was it his 6th? He wasn't sure—he'd lost count. He hadn't been looking forward to it. But part of him, even if he didn't like to admit it, was glad for the autumn term to start. It'd give himself something ordinary to concentrate on.

Nothing strange had happened in the past week or so since his birthday. But that day's events were never too far from his thoughts. Sometimes, he really did wonder whether he'd gone mad. He would rather he was just going loopy—it would be a much simpler explanation than the real one. He had a feeling there was more to come. It was unnerving not knowing when it would happen, or what it might be.

Thankfully, his first day at school was at least keeping his mind off things. He planned to just keep quiet and bury himself in his in the day. The school was called St

Barnaby's. He had to get a couple of buses to get there. He'd been to view the school before he registered and so knew what to expect as he walked up the drive. The main building was large and old—it had been some kind of Victorian manor house before it had been converted into a school in the mid-1900s. A few small and more modern buildings were dotted about the grounds. There had been a slightly creepy and mysterious air about the place, the first time he had been there with his dad. He had had a strong feeling, as they had walked down the gloomy corridors, that there was going to be something lurking around the corners and in the shadows. That had been in the summer holidays though, when the place was virtually empty, bar a couple of staff members. Now that the place was packed full of other kids running around, shouting and messing about, it was too noisy to be mysterious.

Dylan's form tutor was called Miss Straithwhite. She was strict, but nothing unbearable. She had white hair and thin wire framed glasses, which she had a habit of looking over at the pupils in a menacing manner. She made a point of making the class aware of Dylan's presence, but didn't make him stand up and introduce himself to the whole class, as had been his experience when starting at other schools. He was grateful for this and used the opportunity to keep a low profile during the day. He did notice one girl giving him some odd looks during the register. She was sitting a couple of rows to his left. She had a very serious face with dark eyes and thick brown hair. She kept looking at Dylan with an expression of curiosity he did his best to ignore.

At lunch time he found couple of steps in the playground leading to a bricked up door, out of the way of the other children. He was munching a sandwich and studying the leaves on the ground when a pair of shoes entered his vision. He looked up. It was the girl who had been staring at him.

'Hello,' she said in a strong, well-spoken voice.

'Hi. I'm Dylan.' He didn't look at her or get up.

'I know. You're in my form class. I'm Audrey. Do you mind if I join you?' She sat down beside him without waiting for a reply.

She asked him what sort of things he liked. She didn't ask him any questions about his family or where he'd been living before and so on, which he liked. He told her how much he loved reading fantasies and adventures that took you to strange places. Audrey approved, nodding seriously, although she wasn't so fond of fiction herself. She much preferred books on science and philosophy she said. She couldn't quite get a handle on things that were all made up.

Before long, the bell for the end of lunch rang and they went in to their classes. Audrey made a point of trying to sit next to Dylan for the rest of their classes that day.

It looked like he had made a new friend, and he wasn't really sure if he had all that much choice in the matter.

After school had finished Dylan was walking down St George's Walk on his way to the bus stop to get home. There weren't many people around. Only a couple of elderly shoppers and a mother pushing her child in a buggy.

Dylan walked slowly, not paying much attention to anything. He found himself stopping and looking into the window of Mr Ebenezer's bookshop. It looked as closed as it did the first time he'd been there. He thought about Mr Ebenezer's face staring at him from the post-box. It made him feel slightly sick. He felt tempted to run. Had it really happened? Surely he was just a harmless old man. Not sure exactly what he was going to do, Dylan felt he needed to confront Mr Ebenezer in some way. Swallowing loudly, he slowly pushed open the shop door.

There was no music this time. But everything else was the same—the same dim light and books piled precariously at every angle. Mr Ebenezer was visible straight away, standing behind the counter. Dylan froze and braced himself. But Mr Ebenezer showed no sign of awareness, despite the bell above the door having tinkled as he had come in. He had a book in one hand, held open in front of him. He was studying it intently. Dylan couldn't see the title from where he was standing.

Dylan looked around at the rest of the shop. It didn't look like there were any other customers, though it was hard to tell. Anyone could be concealed behind a passage in the maze of books.

He walked up to the counter and plucked up his courage.

'Excuse me, Mr Ebenezer...' he said.

Still lost in the words of the book, Mr Ebenezer didn't move. Dylan coughed slightly and repeated himself a little louder.

'Oh, who do we have here?' said Mr Ebenezer, looking up and readjusting his glasses with his free hand. 'Why, if it isn't young Master Thompson.' He closed the book and placed it in a drawer behind the counter. His tone of voice was genial, and he didn't exactly look hostile. Dylan relaxed slightly. Maybe that had been in his head. Or it had been a trick of some kind.

'Have you remembered which book it was you were looking for?'

'Yes... Yes, I have.'

What was he saying? He hadn't come in looking for a book.

'Excellent!' Mr Ebenezer clapped his hands together as if he meant business. He leant down and pulled a huge leather bound book out from under the counter, placing it on the surface with a hefty thump and causing a puff of dust to rise.

'Let's have the title then,' said Mr Ebenezer waving away the dust. 'Or the author first, if you wish.'

He looked expectantly at Dylan.

'Umm…' Dylan thought fast. *'Unusual Land Animals of No Small Consequence.'* Where had that come from? Mr Ebenezer would never believe that. But to his surprise Mr Ebenezer looked delighted.

'Well! A rarity—a book I have not heard of! Marvellous. Now let me guess the author. Hmm… McWronikle?'

Dylan shook his head. His stomach turned. Surely, he would be rumbled.

'No? Then maybe Gaius Seluvio?'

Dylan shook his head again.

'Broughton, Welfyon? Not Pemberton?'

'Umm… no, sorry. Not them,' said Dylan apologetically.

'Who could this mysterious writer *be*? How exciting!' Mr Ebenezer seemed to be talking more to himself than to Dylan. 'Now, dear boy, you mustn't keep me in suspense. What name does this author go by?'

'Er, Hibbleton. Yes, that's it. Ignatius Hibbleton.' Dylan crossed his fingers, hoping Mr Ebenezer didn't start getting suspicious.

'Hibbleton? Ignatius Hibbleton. I've heard of Henry Hibbleton, but never an Ignatius Hibbleton. Let's see if he's in stock. I can't keep track of everything you see.'

Mr Ebenezer opened the huge book about a third of

the way through and started flicking speedily through the pages. It must be a catalogue of all the books in the shop, thought Dylan. He peered a little closer. All the entries were in tiny script—there were easily about a hundred entries per page, and, judging by the size of the book, maybe a couple of thousand pages. There were certainly a lot of books in the shop, but surely there couldn't be quite as many as there were in the catalogue.

'Ah, here we are!' said Mr Ebenezer excitedly, running a finger down one side of the page where the authors' names were listed alphabetically by surname. 'Hartsman, Henchley, Hendle, Hibs... Hibbleton! Ignatius Hibbleton...*Unusual Land Animals of No Small Consequence*. Well, well. You are in luck Master Thompson.'

Dylan was dumbfounded. How could a book he had made up on the spot be in the catalogue? But he leaned over and looked to where Mr Ebenezer's finger was pointing in the book. It was there alright.

'So— now the task is to find the thing. If it is in the catalogue, it is in the shop. But I'm afraid I must tell you, there is no order to the books, outside of the catalogue. So you'll have to hunt for the book in all these piles. You may be lucky and find it quickly, or you may find it after much searching, or even not at all. It is, as I say, definitely there somewhere. But you will only find it if it wants you to. Right now though, I'm closing shop, so you'll have to leave. Come back on Thursday after your schooling.

If you help me with some bits and bobs—cataloguing the new books and whatnot, I will let you have the book free of charge. Though I must warn you, you may have to come back a few times, or even many, before you find it. So... That's settled. I shall see you Thursday.'

Mr Ebenezer didn't seem to think that Dylan had a choice in the matter. He was too shell-shocked to disagree and let himself be ushered out of the shop.

'I'll be seeing you on Thursday, Master Thompson,' Dylan heard Mr Ebenezer saying as he walked away from the shop, not quite sure what had just happened.

4

DYLAN WOKE FROM a restless sleep. He had been
dreaming of carrying a heavy canvas bag that was
getting heavier and heavier as he stumbled through
darkness, until he could barely even drag it. He had been
dragging it for a long time. He had no idea of where he
was, or where he was going. Something in the bag had
moved suddenly, causing him to wake. He reached over
and checked his alarm clock. It read 3.23 am.

Something didn't feel right. His head was fuzzy. Not
with sleep, but there was a kind of pins and needles
sensation in his brain, like TV static was passing through
it. He sat up in bed and the feeling lessened slightly. It
seemed like it was a signal, coming from somewhere
outside of the house. He pulled off the bedcovers and
slid out of bed, walking slowly to the window. He lifted
the curtain slightly and peeked out at the orange lamp-lit
street below. A passing fox stopped in the middle of the
road. Its eyes lit up like torches before it scurried off into
the darkness.

It wasn't cold, but Dylan shivered. He could still feel

the fuzzy signal tugging at his mind from somewhere down there, in the street. Thinking about the strange things that had been happening, Dylan decided he wasn't going outside. He told himself to be sensible. He had been having a bad dream, and was out of sorts, that was all. He climbed back into his bed and closed his eyes. He lay there for a couple of minutes trying to empty his thoughts. It was no use. The strange feeling in his head had become stronger.

He got out of bed and went downstairs. It was unusually quiet. Not just in the house, but outside too. Whenever he had woken up in the night before, there was usually some noise—police sirens, the occasional car swooping past. But this silence felt thick, dense and threatening. He found some Paracetamol in one of the kitchen cupboards, poured himself a glass of water and swallowed a tablet.

Passing the front door on his way back, he could feel the strange signal in his head growing in intensity, pulling him towards the door. He couldn't fight it. He put his shoes on and unlocked the door quietly, slipping out into the night.

In the street, he had no hesitation as to which direction he should be headed. The pull on his mind was too great. He turned left and started walking. The night was warm and he was comfortable in his pyjamas. It was still strangely quiet. Even at this time of night there was usually the odd sound of a car going by, or the rattling of a train in the distance.

He walked further down the street, to a particularly darkened corner and came to a stop at the entrance to an alley covered thickly by trees. He had never noticed this alley before. His eyes strained to see anything in the dim light. Although he couldn't make anything out, he could tell that the source of whatever was calling him was down there. Warily, he put one foot in front of the other and proceeded into the alley. A short way down he stopped. He could see something in the shadows, something pale. It could be a person. Whatever it was, it was very still.

'Hello,' he called out.

There was no reply, but in response the static in his brain rushed through him like waves. He moved closer to the figure for a better look. The hairs stood up on his neck. In front of him was what looked like an oversized egg balanced on something wrapped in a raincoat. Kneeling in front of him, motionless, was the creature he had seen on his birthday.

'Rollo!' shouted Dylan. His excitement soon became concern when Rollo still didn't move and made no sign of reply.

Maybe he was sleeping? But it seemed unlikely—why would he have chosen to have a sleep in a dark alley in a reality that wasn't his own? Dylan reached out to touch what he thought was Rollo's shoulder. To his horror, Rollo's head rolled straight off, landing in Dylan's arms like a heavy egg. The static in Dylan's brain cleared immediately. Distraught, Dylan stood there clutching the head, not knowing what to do. Had he killed him?

In a daze, he carefully wrapped Rollo's body and head in the coat and lifted it in his arms. It was surprisingly light.

Once he left the alley, he kept an eye out, very conscious of how suspicious it would look if anyone, glancing out of a window, saw a boy in pyjamas carrying something big in an old coat. Careful not to drop Rollo or make a sound, he walked as quickly as he could. Back in the house, he crept quietly up the stairs and back to his room, pausing in the doorway and listening for any signs of his dad having woken. A reassuringly long snore dutifully echoed down the hall from Jim's room. There was no danger of him waking up when he was like that.

Carefully, he put the large egg shaped head and body on his bed. Was he dead? What else could he be? Yet how could he possibly tell? He didn't understand where Rollo was from or what he was, so he certainly couldn't know for sure how things worked for... *what*ever Rollo was. For all he knew, Rollo's body just needed to be put back together correctly. Or maybe creatures like him just disconnected when they slept.

He'd have to keep him hidden. Carefully, he gathered

Rollo up in the coat again and placed him in the bottom of his wardrobe, covering him in a sheet.

Back in bed, he fell straight into a strange deep sleep, noticing just before he slipped out of consciousness that the fuzz had completely cleared from his head.

As soon as he woke up, he jumped out of bed and went to the wardrobe. He pulled out the coat containing Rollo. He picked up the head in his hands. It felt like soapstone. He held it up to his ear, though what he expected to hear inside it, he couldn't say.

There was no sign of life in the head or the body. The only feeling Dylan got touching Rollo was that he didn't belong here, that he wasn't of this world. Cold, but not clammy, not what he imagined any body, dead or alive, would ever feel like. Strangely, he'd broken into bits like a statue or a doll. His dad called him down to breakfast. Quickly, he placed Rollo back into the coat and hid him in the wardrobe, beneath a sheet.

His mind was in a wild spin all day. Audrey had taken to sitting next to him in lessons as much as possible. She was getting frustrated with him for being even more distracted than usual. She had been trying to tell him about an amazing wildlife documentary she had seen on TV the night before, but didn't get much of a response.

At lunch time, when Dylan still seemed to be in a very funny mood, Audrey decided it was time to confront him. She was not the sort of person who could stand not knowing what was going on. They were sitting in the corner of the Quad, a concrete square between the main school buildings, on some steps that led up to a passage that in turn led up to a mysteriously blocked door. They had just finished their lunch.

'So,' said Audrey decisively. 'What's up with you?'

Dylan stared at the ground.

'Come on, tell me.'

'There's something at home. In my wardrobe… I want to show you…it's weird. Awesome.' He didn't know what else to say. There was too much to explain. She just looked at him and nodded. He knew she was someone he could trust.

The lessons dragged, fear followed by confusion swept over him. He kept seeing strange images—Rollo, Rollo's head, the bear in the field, rain frozen like plastic, a strange blackness giving birth to a monster the size of an elephant.

'What planet are you on?' asked one of the teachers making everyone laugh. Audrey gave his hand a squeeze.

As soon as they entered the house, they went straight to his bedroom. He pointed to the wardrobe in the corner.

'It's in there.'

He knelt down and opened the door. Audrey came and

knelt beside him. Dylan pushed trousers and shirts out of the way and took off the bed sheet that was covering Rollo's coat. He paused and looked at Audrey. 'Please, whatever you think, please don't think I've gone nuts.'

She looked at him very seriously, 'Dylan, you are far from nuts. Have you actually paid attention to the other boys in our class? *They're* nuts. Now, get on with it.'

Dylan breathed in and held his breath. It was now or never, he thought. He reached into the wardrobe and opened up Rollo's coat.

There was nothing there! The coat was empty.

'But… where is it, where's his head? Where has he gone?'

'Who's he?'

He began explaining. To his relief, the words just tumbled out. He told her almost everything, right from the beginning—the snake in the plughole, the strange visions that he'd been seeing and the pins and needles sensation, the events on his birthday, meeting Rollo, right up until the previous night when he had found Rollo's body. The only part he'd missed out was the moment he'd seen Mr Ebenezer in the post-box and the following events with that boy, Pete. Audrey didn't say anything while he told her his story. She had a look of extreme concentration and took a few moments to process it, once he had finished.

'Hmmmm,' she said, going quiet.

'Hmmmm? Is that all you're going to say?'

'What can I say?'

'You do believe me? Say you believe it all really happened.'

'I can't just say I believe it *all* happened.'

'I'm not lying!' Dylan raised his voice defensively.

'I didn't say you were lying.'

'But if you don't believe those things happened, you must think I'm lying.'

'I kind of believe you Dylan. There is something going on—something awesome.' Her eyes met his. He looked down at his hands.

'Phone me if anything else weird happens. Promise.'

'Promise.'

After she had gone, Dylan sat down on his bed and held Rollo's coat. It *had* happened. And the coat was evidence. It's not as if he had sleepwalked out into the street and picked up a random coat that happened to be lying outside. He wondered were Rollo was now. He hoped he wasn't dead. And that he was ok, wherever he was.

5

IT WAS A good thing that he'd told Audrey about Rollo, the only good thing he had to hang on to. The next day at school, she didn't say anything about what he had told her the night before. Instead they talked about all manner of other things. Starting from something Audrey had read, about a theory that there were endless different worlds where all the different possibilities were carried out. So there was one world where you tied your shoe laces properly and carried on with your day as normal and another where you hadn't tied them properly, which had resulted in them coming loose and you tripping into a person who turned out to be an international spy who decides to entrust an important document to you to deliver to a top secret organisation. They imagined realities where gravity had stopped working and any-thing not fixed to the ground floated off into the sky.

It was the day that Mr Ebenezer had asked him to come and help in the shop, so after school Dylan got the bus into town instead of heading home. He hadn't told his dad that he was going to help in a bookshop, but

Mark Bardwell

instead had said that he had joined the chess club at school. He wasn't completely sure why he had lied about it, but it seemed easier that way.

Mr Ebenezer was sitting at the counter and reading.

'Master Thompson, good day to you,' he said, looking up as he heard the bell above the door tinkle. 'It's very good of you to keep our appointment. You may sit down for a moment,' he said nodding towards a chair in the corner.

He sat down waiting for Mr Ebenezer to speak, but he seemed to have gone back to reading his book. He must be finishing a paragraph, or maybe he was at the end of a chapter. Dylan looked around the shop. Nothing much had changed since he had last been there, at least not obviously. The hundreds of books were still piled precariously to create towering passageways. They looked like they hadn't been disturbed in a long time.

He wondered what he was doing there. What was the name of the book he'd made up, the one that turned out to actually exist? *Animals That Never Went Anywhere*? No, something like *Unusual Land Trains*. That didn't sound quite right either. Well, it'd be interesting to find it. In a strange way, he felt partly responsible for its existence. He looked back at Mr Ebenezer who was completely absorbed in the book, his whole body bent forward and his shock of wavy white hair obscuring his face. Dylan must have been sitting there for ten or fifteen minutes.

40

It seemed very likely that Mr Ebenezer had forgotten that he was there. He would have to say something.

Dylan coughed the sort of cough that Miss Straithwhite used in class to get people's attention. No reaction came from the mop of hair hovering over the book.

'Um, Mr Ebenezer.'

Mr Ebenezer's head didn't move. He only raised a finger in the air, telling Dylan to wait.

A couple more minutes passed before Mr Ebenezer finally raised his eyes and stared at Dylan. 'What are you doing still sitting there, boy?' he said sternly.

'Well, you told me to sit here... so I have been,' Dylan said, a little defiantly.

'Humph. Never mind all that. Right. Look sharp.'

Mr Ebenezer led Dylan around the corner of one row of books, took a left and then a right and another right. As they went along, Dylan took note of the length of the passageways and the directions. They seemed a lot longer than they should be, considering how small the shop looked from the outside. Maybe it went further back than he thought.

'Ok!' said Mr Ebenezer, stopping suddenly. 'Let's call this 'row A',' he pointed at the row of books on the left, 'and this row, 'row C',' indicating the books on the right. Dylan wondered where row B was, but didn't have time to ask as Mr Ebenezer went rapidly on.

'What I want you to do is move the first ten deep

section from row A, starting at the corner and transfer them to the wall, moving across to row C, forming row D. Then, please, move twelve deep from row C, starting where row C meets row D, and place them diagonally down the way we have just come, between row A and row C to form row E.

'But if I do that, I'll block my way out!'

'No, you won't,' he said rolling his eyes as if Dylan was being unbearably slow. He pointed at Dylan's chest, 'You may, of course, read the spines—how else would you find the book you are seeking—but I forbid you to look inside any of the books. I will know if you have done that.' He scuttled off down the passage and around the corner. As he went out of sight, he called out. 'Don't forget to keep your eyes peeled for *Unusual Land Animals of No Small Consequence* as you go along, Master Thompson. If you don't keep your eyes sharp, you're likely to never find it.'

For a moment Dylan just stood there, bewildered. Ten deep. Presumably, he meant ten books along. Well, he might as well start. It wouldn't be the end of the world, if he got it wrong. And if he did trap himself in, he would just have to push the books over to get out, if the worst came to the worst. Something was telling him he should try not to anger Mr Ebenezer.

He got to work moving the books from row A. He counted ten books down and started moving them to the wall. As he did so, he took care to scan the titles of the books. It was hard not to stop and look through them. They were all rather old hardbacks—there was nothing modern, or anything that looked like it was from anytime in the last thirty years or so. There were so many books that Dylan's desire to stop and read quickly disappeared. It would take too long. Soon he was only stopping to sneeze every now and then from all the dust he unsettled. As he fell into a rhythm, he lost all track of time. He kept going automatically until, to his surprise, he had moved the books he needed from row A and had formed row E. In doing so, he'd also created an entrance to another passageway in the space from where he had moved books. That would hopefully be the way out.

He set to work moving the books from row C. He soon fell into the same rhythm of picking up the books, scanning the titles and then placing them in their new row. As he revealed the space behind row C, he found it was unusually dark. It must be a dead end, completely closed off by the other books. But it was strange that no light got in there as the books didn't reach the ceiling.

A short while later, as Dylan's thoughts had drifted into his subconscious, he nearly jumped out of his skin when he picked up a very thick book to reveal the head of a llama on the other side of the row of books. Amazed, he took a step back. The llama was staring him right in the eye with a mischievous look. It was chewing on something, and what looked like book pages were sticking out of its mouth. Suddenly he got that feeling of pins and needles. Confused, he turned around and called out for Mr Ebenezer.

There was no reply.

'Mr Ebenezer, there's a llama behind row C. It's eating your books!'

Still no reply.

Dylan turned around. There was no sign of the llama and the pins and needles had gone. Maybe it had just vanished, like all the other weird things he had seen. Nervously, Dylan carried on moving the books. He was worried the llama would turn up again and decide to chew his fingers instead of the books.

Maybe he *was* going mad. How long had he been in the shop? He had completely lost track of time now. The battery on his mobile had run out. He wished he had remembered to put his watch on. It felt like he had been there a very long time. His dad would definitely be worrying. But he felt compelled to carry on. The llama showed no signs of turning up again and Dylan started moving faster, barely taking in the titles of the books.

A while later he was done. He stood staring into the dead end, he had revealed. It was still unimaginably dark. It didn't make any sense—there was a light directly above where he stood and there was no reason it would not reach the area of the shop in front of him. Looking into it made him very uneasy. Turning, he hurried into the new passageway that had been revealed by opening up row A. He ran quickly down the passage and turned instinctively at the junctions he came upon, guessing the direction back to the front of the shop. He didn't seem to be getting anywhere. He soon had to stop to think it through. Surely the shop wasn't large enough for him to get properly lost?

As he stopped, his eyes settled on a book in front of him. The title was *The Day the World Decided to Do Without Gravity*. Intrigued, he eased the book out from the pile and held it in his hands. It wouldn't hurt to have a look, he thought—it was only a book, after all. As his fingers touched the edge of the cover, he felt a shadow fall over him.

He looked up to discover Mr Ebenezer peering down at him, standing slightly too close for comfort. He hadn't even heard him coming.

'Master Thompson, will you kindly replace the book to where you discovered it. Nothing must be moved unnecessarily. Heaven knows what you thought you were doing in this part of the shop. Now, follow me immediately.'

Dylan slid the book back into its place without saying anything.

Mr Ebenezer nodded and turned on his heel and made off at a brisk pace. Dylan followed, finding it hard to keep up. He was sure they were going the way that he'd just come, back to the dark corner, but soon they were at the front of the shop again.

'Well, Master Thompson. I thank you for your assistance. I'm sorry you didn't find your book. Well, if it's meant to be, it will find *you* at some point I'm sure, if you are incapable of finding it yourself. I must close the shop now, so be a good young man and run home to your tea.'

Mr Ebenezer was fussing with some papers on his desk. Dylan sighed. He'd be glad to get out of there. He went to the door. As he opened it, he turned round and said, 'Mr Ebenezer, can I just ask you something? The corner of the shop behind row C—it's completely dark. But, well, it shouldn't be. There is plenty of light to get to it. I just wondered if you have ever noticed it?'

Mr Ebenezer eyed Dylan. His face held a trace of the look that had frightened him the day he had run into that boy Pete.

'Nonsense! Take your childish imagination out of my shop at once! Can't you see that I'm busy?'

Dylan left in a hurry. He had a slightly sick feeling in his stomach and he was relieved to be out in the fresh air. There was definitely something not quite right about Mr Ebenezer and his shop. It would probably be best if he avoided going back.

When he got home, he crept in gingerly. He must have

been at the shop for a few hours. It certainly felt like it. He walked into the kitchen to get a glass of water. His dad was in there making a cup of tea.

'Hello, chap. Were you playing speed chess?' Jim asked, 'I wasn't expecting you back so early.'

'Why? What time is it?'

'A quarter past four. Are you OK, Dylan? You look a little pale.'

6

Later that evening, Dylan was upstairs doing his homework at his desk. Concentrating on his maths was helping put Mr Ebenezer and his shop out of his mind. Taking a break, he plugged his mobile phone into its charger.

As soon as he switched the phone on the message tone peeped. It was a text message from Audrey.

Are you OK Dylan? I had a weird feeling after school. Probably nothing, I know, but I thought, I'd better check.

Dylan just texted back: I'm OK thanks. Odd afternoon, but everything's normal now

Dylan got back on with his Maths. A minute later the phone peeped again. Another text from Audrey: What kind of odd?

He sighed. Audrey would have to wait. He put his mobile phone down and continued with his studying.

About ten minutes later there was another peep. It didn't sound the same as the last one. He picked up the phone. There was no message symbol on the display. He put it back down. It was probably a sound from outside.

Again that weird sound. Now it sounded more like a whistle than a peep. It was definitely coming from somewhere in his bedroom. One of the doors of his wardrobe had opened slightly, just a crack.

'Pss,' came a voice from inside. 'Dylan. Over here.'

'Rollo?' Excitement and nervousness were bubbling inside him. Could he really be alive? Or what if it wasn't Rollo?

'It's me, Rollovkarghjicznilegogh,' whispered the voice.

'Rollo!' said Dylan more loudly than he meant to, springing up. He didn't want his dad to hear.

'Yes, yes. I've already said it was me.'

'Are you going to come out of the wardrobe?'

'Umm. I would, but it appears that I'm naked. Have you seen my coat anywhere?'

Dylan looked around the room—it was at the foot of his bed. 'Got it!'

'Well, bring it here then!'

Dylan took the coat over to the wardrobe and placed it in the bony hand that came out.

'Ah, much better.' For a few minutes he seemed to be shuffling around inside the wardrobe. Then he pushed open the doors.

'Dylan! A pleasure to make your acquaintance again!' he said loudly spreading out his arms dramatically.

'Shhh!' Dylan put a finger to his lips. 'My dad is downstairs. We don't want him to hear you.'

Rollo lowered his voice. 'Don't we? Yes, it's probably for the best. Although, who knows if he could see me. You're the only person who's seen me in this reality so far. Though, I guess, I've barely spent any time here.'

'What happened to you, Rollo?' Dylan asked softly.

Rollo started pacing up and down.

'Let me think. What happened to me, what happened to me... I don't know, I'm afraid. I was travelling back to this reality—purposefully this time—aiming to get near you. There must be something funny going on in your brain, by the way. It was like a beacon, and it shouldn't be. Anyway, I've digressed. Not that there is much to digress from. I got here OK. I was in an alley which I presume is near here. I'm usually very alert having slipped, it alerts the body like nothing else, but I felt immensely sleepy and had to have a sit down. It seems I drifted off. And woke up in your wardrobe. Why did you put me in your wardrobe? Is it something you usually do to guests in RTH-0709?'

Rollo stopped pacing and looked at Dylan. Although Rollo didn't have any eyes, Dylan could definitely tell when Rollo was looking at him. It was almost like being prodded physically.

'RTH-0709?'

'Ah yes, sorry. You will be new to this, your reality being untapped until now. RTH-0709 are the co-ordinates assigned to this reality by the Intrapelatio Union.

They haven't gotten round to giving it a name yet. There's no rush to really—this place is being kept top secret at the moment, what with all that's going on. If you give secret things names, they always seem to get out sooner. Though these days nothing in the Intrapelatio seems to be kept secret for very long. Anyway, I'm rambling. I really would like to know how I came to be in your wardrobe?'

Dylan was more interested in all the stuff Rollo had been saying about reality and secrets. He'd have to ask in a moment.

'Well, I thought you might be dead.'

Rollo cocked his head, but said nothing. Dylan went on, 'When I found you, your head fell off in my hands. I thought you were dead. Well, *might* be dead. I've not really any experience with your... type. So I hid you in my wardrobe. I couldn't leave you out where my dad could see. How would I explain it to him? I don't really know what's going on myself. And then you vanished. And now you're back again.' Dylan paused. 'Is it normal for you to lose your head like that?'

'No, it's not normal. You were right to think I was dead. We only disassemble like that when we die.'

Rollo seemed lost in thought. Dylan waited for him to go on. He'd have to have a think about it too, if he'd woken up in someone's wardrobe, only to be told that he'd been dead, had vanished and then re-appeared, inexplicably and alive again.

'Never mind,' said Rollo, quite cheerfully, 'I'm certainly not dead now, so there's not much point in worrying about it. I just hope it doesn't happen again, any time soon.'

A knock on the door made him jump. He looked at Rollo in alarm, but he was already ducking down behind the bed, out of sight.

The knock came again. Dylan turned back to his desk so it looked like he was still studying.

'Yeah?' he called out as casually as he could.

The door opened and his dad's head popped in.

'It's nearly nine o'clock, Dylan. You can stop the homework for this evening, can't you? Our comedy is on in a moment.'

It was Dylan and Jim's favourite TV comedy and they always made a point of watching together. Jim would start suspecting something was up if he didn't go down to watch it. Rollo would be OK for half an hour. Hopefully he wouldn't vanish again.

He got up, switched his lamp off and followed his father down the stairs. It was a funny episode, but Dylan was distracted.

When it was over he told Jim that he was going to read in bed and said good night. He found Rollo stretched out behind his bed with hands behind his head. He appeared to be sleeping but it was hard to tell because he didn't seem to breathe. Maybe he was some kind of robot. Tentatively, Dylan shook Rollo by the shoulder, hoping very much that he wasn't going to 'disassemble' again. To his relief, Rollo stirred and sat upright.

'Sorry about that. I thought I'd have a snooze while you were gone. I can't remember the last time I was so tired.'

He stretched his arms out above his head and stood up.

'It's occurred to me Dylan—what with this reality being so innocent and untapped, and you being but a youngling—you're probably quite confused. So first things first. I guess I should explain some things. Maybe it'd be best if you asked some questions. It might not occur to me what things you will or won't be aware of. So, are you ready to fire away?'

Dylan sat down on his bed and nodded.

'I guess the first thing would be... well, what are you?'

'Ah, a nice easy question. I am an intelligence gatherer of sorts. An investigator. Freelance. I travel between realities keeping an eye on things, investigating particular situations for my clients. The Intrapelatio Union is my most common customer, but I do work for independent organisations on occasion. At my own discretion, of course. I've turned down quite a few dodgy sounding assignments, I can tell you.'

'Oh... Ok... I meant really, what sort of *being* are you? There's no one like you in our reality. Are you... a robot?'

'A robot!' Rollo exclaimed, quite offended. 'My goodness, do you really think I look like a robot? Why do squidgy fleshy beings always think something's up because our bones are on the outside? It makes sense doesn't it? You can't cut and scrape me so easily. Our bones are almost as hard as diamond. Much more sensible having them external. A robot!' Rollo shook his head disbelievingly.

'I'm really sorry.' Dylan was flustered. He hadn't meant any offence. 'This is all very new to me. So, what sort of being are you?'

'Hmm... I guess you can't be blamed too much. I am a jelli being'

Dylan couldn't help letting out a small laugh. 'A jelly bean?'

'*Jelli*. J-E-L-L-I. A jelli being. Are all younglings so immature in RTH-0709? If you're quite ready to continue, I'll answer your questions.'

'Sorry,' said Dylan, straightening his face. 'So. Do jelli beings come from an Earth, but in a different reality?'

'No—we are from far across the galaxy. Earth is quite uninhabitable in Psarphle—that's the name of our reality.'

'My friend Audrey was talking about a theory she's heard. According to this theory there's a different reality for every possibility. There's one reality where you decide to go to the cinema, and one where you don't and all these different things that could happen exist side by side in different realities. Is it like that? Could you travel to a reality where, umm… say, I'd become the youngest ever Prime Minister?'

'Prime Minister? I don't know what that is, but it sounds quite silly. No. I can't move between realities like the ones you describe. There are many theories about the possibility of there being infinitely more realities than the ones we know about, covering all eventualities. But if there are, we don't know about them.'

'So, what are the different realities that you are talking about?'

Dylan was trying his best to concentrate. There wasn't much chance he would understand everything that Rollo said, but it was important to get as much of an idea as possible.

'They are different realities that all occur within the same galaxy. They've all got solar systems and planets and so on, but the life on the planets only occurs in one reality each. At least, as far as we know. So there is only one reality in which there are jelli beings, one with human beings, one with slofarbs and so on. There are five hundred and fifty-seven known realities, five hundred and six of which have joined to form the Intrapelatio Union in order to keep peace and order. Although beings travel between realities, and do spend periods of time in those other than their own, they can't settle there. All intra-reality travel is strictly regulated. Terrible things happen if you spend too much time in another reality.'

'What sort of terrible things?'

'Hmmm… I don't think we'd have time to go into it now. And I doubt you'd sleep, if I told you some of the things that have happened in some realities. Though, I will say, there used to be five hundred and fifty-eight known realities. A reality called Raphire was invaded around forty of your years ago. An army of beings called Tefnin were trying to escape the war and famine that was raging in their own reality. They believed they had developed technology that would enable them to live in Raphire without causing problems. The Parbols of Raphire were peaceful creatures and weren't equipped to defend themselves against an army of the Tefnins' size. The Tefnin didn't fight any more than necessary—that's not what they were there for. Everything was fine for a year or so. It lasted a lot longer than anyone would have imagined without anything going wrong. But then the whole of Raphire vanished without warning. No more Raphire. This has never happened before or since. There certainly isn't anything where its co-ordinates were. We don't know if the Tefnin were destroyed, or they simply ended up elsewhere. There was a department set up at the Union to investigate the situation and determine whether the Tefnin simply ceased to exist or if they moved on, mutated... Well, whatever happened to them, they're still investigating and not much the wiser than they were then they started...Do you remember that creature you saw the day we met?'

Dylan nodded.

'Zounds if I know how it got here, but if it had been left here to run amok, RTH-0709 could have suffered a very similar fate to Raphire. Those horned men that took it back were *slarpups*. They were members of their police force. They are part of the Intrapelatio Union, but they're a shady bunch and not to be trusted. You're lucky they turned up, though. But it is very worrying that the creature got here somehow. *And* that the slarpups were able to follow. We don't really want *them* snooping around a freshly tapped reality.'

Rollo paused. Dylan didn't say anything for a while. It was mind bending to think there were so many wild things happening that no one knew about and not just in outer space.

'So, have you come back to explore RTH-0709?'

'No. It's not ready for that—it would be months before anything like that could happen. And it wouldn't be my job. My general line of work involves political situations between tapped realities. It would be a team of Union scientists and diplomats that would come here first. And you couldn't just turn up and say, 'Hello, we're form another reality to have a look around'. But nothing like that is planned at the moment. There are much bigger and immediate worries.'

'What worries? And why *are* you here? You didn't actually answer my question.'

'To have a look around. There's something odd going on at the moment. I think RTH-0709 is linked somehow.'

Rollo seemed to have become contemplative. A seriousness had crept into his voice.

'The time that I ended up here by accident, that's troubling for starters. Just the fact of ending up somewhere by accident for an experienced intra-reality traveller such as myself is worrying, but to end up somewhere untapped… Well, you can imagine.'

Dylan couldn't really imagine, but he nodded his head anyway.

'And I later found out that at the same time one of the sanctuaries had sealed itself. This has never happened before. There are seven sanctuaries, you see, which are like pockets between realities. There is nothing in them. They are a dark and empty space. And they will remain so unless they encounter a particularly strong mind of powerful imagination. Beings with sufficient imagination are able to shape new realities in these places. The headquarters of the Intrapelatio Union is in one of these pockets, or rather was. The environment and buildings were made purely from the greatest imaginations gathered from all realities. It is a neutral space between realities in which democracy can reign unhindered, no room for evil dictators. To get to the point though—one of the sanctuaries has sealed itself from the inside. Either the space has developed a will of its own or, more likely, someone has managed to seal themselves in. And just when they sealed themselves in, I found myself pulled into RTH-0709 when I was on my way somewhere else entirely. As was that creature we saw.'

'So you think my reality is linked to what's going on?'

'Yes. I mean, there are no other leads at the moment. No one knows who has sealed themselves in the sanctuary, or what they could be up to. One thing everyone knows, though—it means grave danger. Whatever is happening, it has to be stopped. But great care must be taken.'

Rollo was silent.

'I think I'm going to need some time to process this,' said Dylan.

Rollo placed a hand firmly on his shoulder.

'I'm afraid, Dylan, that time is something we simply don't have.'

Something like an electric shock jolted through Dylan from Rollo's hand and shot through his body. He tried to say something, but his jaw was firmly clamped shut. Rollo leaned closer and said calmly, 'No need to worry.'

A dark cloud suddenly appeared across the room in front of the curtains. With a tremendous pull, Dylan and Rollo were sucked inside.

7

DARKNESS. He seemed to be nowhere. Nowhere at all. He couldn't feel his body. It was as if only his mind existed. He couldn't sense Rollo's presence. His thoughts spun fast and panic rose. What had Rollo done to him? Where was he? Where was his body? Was he dead? Was Rollo really against him? He couldn't make sense of it. He strained, but…

There was a sucking noise. Suddenly he could feel his body again, his arms, legs toes and hands tingled. He could feel Rollo's grip on his shoulder. Light suddenly appeared, blinding him momentarily. He shook himself free from Rollo and staggered a few steps away.

'What did you do to me?' he called out, fear in his voice. Rollo now seemed sinister. Dylan looked around himself. They appeared to be in a forest clearing on a sunny day. The trees' leaves were vividly green, as was the grass beneath his feet. He was only in socks. There was a faint breeze quietly rustling the leaves. No one else there.

'Where are we?' he asked.

Rollo didn't reply. He was looking at their surroundings as if scoping the place out. Dylan felt a nervous sick feeling in his stomach. The air tasted oddly metallic and the trees, although definitely trees, didn't look like any that he recognised.

'Good,' said Rollo, 'It doesn't look like there's anyone around to have seen us arrive.' He looked at Dylan. 'What are you looking so panicky for?'

'What do you mean?' said Dylan, unbelievingly. 'We were in my bedroom a moment ago, then I seemed to lose my body. And now we're who on Earth knows where!'

'Well, we're not on Earth, that's for sure,' said Rollo, matter of factly. 'I've brought you to see the door to the closed sanctuary. And I wanted to check if the situation has changed.'

'You could have warned me! I was scared half to death. I thought I *was* dead for a moment.'

'I thought it might be more exciting for you this way. It's nothing to worry about. A couple more times slipping and it'll start to feel pretty normal.'

'You can't just make someone travel to another reality without warning. It's… it's horrible! And what if I didn't want to go? And what about when my dad finds I'm missing?'

'Oh, stop fussing. We'll get you back safe and sound, don't you worry. We won't be here too long anyway, I shouldn't think. Follow me.'

Rollo turned and started walking without waiting to make sure Dylan was following. Dylan hesitated for a moment, but on second thoughts Rollo was his only route home. He had to admit it was exciting being in another reality, even if he couldn't quite believe it. He wished he had some shoes on. It wasn't long before Rollo signalled for Dylan to stop. They hid behind a trunk of one of the trees.

'What are we hiding from?' he asked.

'Shhh!' said Rollo 'Quiet. We don't want to be found. There would be a lot of questions if you were seen. No one has seen humans before. They'd soon be asking to see your papers. And as you don't have any, that'd lead to more questions. They'd ask me where I found you and exactly what I'm doing. You'd certainly have a much tougher time getting back.'

'But you're working for them, aren't you? The Intrapelatio Union? So you'd be able to tell them about me.'

Rollo ignored the question. He pointed round the trunk. 'There—look in the middle of the clearing. There is the gateway to the closed sanctuary. Just poke your head out a little and be careful not to be seen. It's heavily guarded.'

Dylan stuck his head out a little. There was indeed a clearing. The sun shone brightly down, making Dylan aware how much the trees had been filtering out the light. In the centre of the clearing was a door. It was a very ordinary looking door. It looked like it could have been the front door of any of the houses on the road he lived on. It was just a wooden door in a frame with ordinary locks and a brass knocker. It even had a letter box. The only thing that made it not ordinary was that it was standing completely unattached to anything in a forest clearing. Dylan wanted to go and look at the other side of the door to see what was there. Standing next to the door was a small smartly dressed man with a very mole like head. He was wearing a monocle and fumbling through his pockets.

'I wouldn't call that a gateway,' whispered Dylan. 'More a misplaced front door. And I thought you said it was heavily guarded?'

'It *is* heavily guarded, Dylan! I'd like to see you try to get past Jeephus there. It's not all down to brute force you know. Doesn't anyone look beyond the immediate in RTH-0709? Honestly. Jeephus is an old friend of mine, but plays it very much by the book. I'm glad it's him here. I'm going to have a word with him. You wait here. Don't move—keep an eye out, and if you are spotted by anyone, do not say anything to them.'

Rollo stepped out from behind the tree and strode towards Jeephus. When they met, Jeephus shook Rollo by the hand with great enthusiasm and they started talking animatedly. Jeephus gestured towards the door. Dylan was too far away to hear what was being said. A few minutes passed and he started daydreaming. After a while, some movement caught his attention from the corner of his eyes. He looked over to where it was. There was an extraordinary looking bird hopping around at his feet. It stared at him with two eyes that were much more like the eyes of a cat than a bird and its legs were furry and ended in paws like those of a cat. The rest of it was more or less birdlike. It was coloured in vivid greens and blues. It continued hopping here and there without ever averting its curious gaze from Dylan.

Dylan laughed. 'You're a strange little creature,' he said. 'We don't have birds like you back in my reality. But I guess I must look just as odd to you. I must be the first human being that you've ever seen.'

The bird froze suddenly and eyed Dylan before darting off into the air and out of sight. He looked back into the clearing. Rollo was walking back towards him. Instead of stopping at the tree, he carried on and beckoned Dylan to join him. Dylan hurried to catch up.

'Neither good news or bad news, Dylan,' said Rollo. 'Jeephus has told me that the Intrapelatio are still at a loss as to what's going on. They have no idea who has locked themselves away inside the sanctuary. Figuring it most likely to be someone of significance to have sufficient imagination to lock a sanctuary, they have run through all reports of missing persons from within the Intrapelatio to see if any such person has gone missing.

They haven't, it seems. Their view is that, as it would be a notable being, they wouldn't go missing without someone noticing. They're being a bit too narrow minded in their search, if you ask me. You'd think they'd have a bit more imagination themselves. Oh, and they haven't found how to get to RTH-0709 yet. They're trying their hardest. I've no idea why they haven't figured it out yet.'

'But *you* know how to get there, don't you? I mean, you came back again *and* knew how to find me. And you know how to take me back, right?'

Rollo stopped suddenly and turned to Dylan.

'No one saw you, did they, while I was talking to Jeephus? You didn't speak to anyone?'

'No.'

'Good.' Rollo turned to carry on.

'Well...' Dylan hesitated.

'Well what?'

'Nothing really. I didn't talk to anyone, just this weird little bird.'

'Bird?' Rollo's voice was serious. It put Dylan on edge.

'Yeah. The birds here are peculiar. It looked half cat.'

'What did you say to it?'

'Oh, nothing much... how we didn't have birds like that in my reality and how I must be the first human being it'd seen.'

'Too much!' said Rollo, continuing to walk. 'I told you

not to talk to anyone. It was quite simple, you know.'

'I didn't think it extended to the local wildlife.'

'Wildlife? There are no birds in this reality. That was most certainly a *grefartchen* you were happy chatting to. He or she would have been quite able to talk back to you. And to tell the Intrapelatio or who knows else that there is a human being from RTH-0709 walking around the area of the closed sanctuary.'

'Well, I wasn't to know,' said Dylan a little sulkily. 'What would they do about it anyway?'

'They'd know that a human had travelled here from RTH-0709. That he had worked out how to get here. Or someone had helped him get here—me! They might start to think you've got something to do with the whole situation. Which means they'll be looking out for you.'

'But you're taking me back aren't you? So they won't find me unless they come back to my reality. And they'll find loads of humans there.'

'But there's nothing to say you'll stay put in your own reality.'

Rollo was leading them towards some rocks, in which appeared to be the entrance to a cave.

'Where else would I go? Where are you taking me now, anyway?' Dylan asked as they entered the cave.

'Somewhere to keep out of trouble for a bit,' said Rollo, once again placing his arm on Dylan's shoulder. The electric shock feeling pulsed through him and he sensed something pulling at them from within the cave. Everything went dark.

Dylan's mind was back in the darkness. It still scared him, even though he expected it this time. It felt like nothing else. It was lonely. Nothing was there but his mind. Maybe this *was* what death was like. Thoughts of his mother suddenly flooded his consciousness. He tried to cry out, but couldn't. An instant later he was back in his bedroom, Rollo was standing beside him with his hand on his shoulder.

'Don't worry,' he said, his voice gentler than normal. 'You'll get used to it.'

'I don't want to get used to it,' said Dylan quietly. 'Aren't there better ways to travel?'

'Slipping is the only way to travel between realities, I'm afraid, young Dylan. You're not needing to slip again any time soon, anyhow. You should get some sleep.'

Fat chance of that, thought Dylan as Rollo walked over to the window and opened it. 'What are you doing now?'

'Research,' said Rollo, sticking a leg out of the window. I might not be back for a few days or so. Keep an eye out for anything unusual. Be sure to make a note of it and tell me when I'm back.'

'OK. But are you sure you wouldn't rather use the front doo-'

Before Dylan could finish his sentence, Rollo had leapt

out of the window. Dylan rushed over to see Rollo's huddled figure hasten down into the street and disappear out of sight.

When Dylan woke up the next day, it wasn't with disbelief. Strange occurrences were starting to feel normal. All the same, he did lie in bed instead of getting up, wondering at the fact that last night he had travelled somewhere that no one in his reality knew existed. He'd seen things that no other human being had seen. As far as he knew. How would Audrey react to this one? He snorted a laugh. A bang came on his door.

'Dylan, you're going to be late,' his dad's voice sounded

During lessons he couldn't concentrate. In geography he'd been so lost in a daydream that it took Mr Groncle a few attempts at getting his attention, much to the class's delight, who were all laughing at the confused and flustered look on Dylan's face. He wasn't surprised when Audrey cornered him at first break.

'Right. What's up this time? What's happened now? You brain doesn't seem to be in the same reality as the rest of us.'

Dylan smiled. 'It wasn't last night, that's for sure.'

Audrey frowned. 'And what does that mean exactly?'

'Just that. Rollo came back. He wasn't dead or vanished... Well, I don't know what. But anyway. You know what we were saying about different realities the other day? Well, it turns out there are different realities—loads. But not in the way we were talking about. They're full of all sorts of different beings. And there's this closed sanctuary place that is all wrong. Which might mean danger. I'm not sure what sort. But Rollo thinks it might be related to RTH-0709. That's why he's back—to investigate.'

'RTH-07- what are you on about, Dylan? None of that makes much sense. Come on, the bell's about to go. Let's go over this again at lunch time—slowly, so I can try to make some sense of this and decide what we need to do.'

'Decide what we need to do? Who put you in charge?'

Just as he said that, the bell rang. Audrey raised an eyebrow, as if to say she didn't need to answer and they made their way to their maths class.

At lunch Dylan sat down with Audrey in the corner of the Quad and went through everything from start to finish, including the previous night's events.

Audrey was silent a moment after Dylan had finished. He twiddled his thumbs a little nervously, waiting to hear what she would say, but he didn't push her.

'You're really weird, Dylan.'

'Thanks.'

'And we're going to investigate this. If there is a link between what's going on in this, what was it... closed sanctuary thing and our reality—we should be finding out what it is exactly.'

'But Rollo said to stay put. He knows a lot more than we do about this. And how would we start investigating—what would we be looking for?'

'Rollo might know more than us. But he doesn't know anything about our reality. We would know when something is odd and sticks out. He might not. I'm not sure we can trust this Rollo person, anyway, from what you've said.'

'What? Why can't we trust him? He brought me back safely, didn't he?'

'Yes, but it was him who took you somewhere that you needed to be taken back from in the first place. And you said that he hadn't told the other people—the people in his union thing.'

'Intrapelatio Union.'

'Yes, Intra-whatever— he hasn't told them that he knows how to get here. Or about you. He didn't even tell his mole-person friend about you. Does someone so secretive sound honest to you, Dylan?'

'Maybe you're right,' said Dylan. He had to admit to himself that the things Audrey pointed out had made him pretty uncomfortable. But he wasn't going to write Rollo off just like that.

'He might have a good reason for not letting on.'

'We don't know, do we?'

'No, we don't, I suppose.'

'So how, exactly, are we going to investigate?'

Audrey frowned and looked thoughtful. 'Is there anything that you've forgotten? Anything you've not told me? Think. It doesn't matter how small—something unusual.'

The question immediately made him think of Mr Ebenezer. He still didn't want to tell Audrey about it. The events with Mr Ebenezer didn't seem real. He wanted to keep it that way and telling Audrey was like admitting that it did happen. The perplexed look on his face gave him away.

'What aren't you telling me?' She raised an eyebrow.

Dylan looked away.

'Dylan...'

He knew it wasn't any use.

'The bookshop...'

'The bookshop? Go on.'

Slowly Dylan started to tell Audrey about Mr Ebenezer and his shop, about the strange incident with the llama and the unnaturally dark corner. And how angry and horrible Mr Ebenezer had become the last time he had seen him.

'That's where we'll go then,' said Audrey when Dylan had finished. 'That's where we'll start. We'll go to the bookshop tomorrow. It's perfect.' Audrey clapped her hands together, stood up and walked away.

He felt a pit in his stomach. He really didn't want to back to that shop. It was Saturday the next day. Maybe he would try and talk her out of it then.

It was very sunny that Saturday morning. Dylan told his dad that he was going into town with Audrey. His dad looked at him, confused as to why he looked so glum.

'Cheer up, chap. It's a glorious sunny day. And a Saturday to boot. Make the most of it before winter starts to creep up on us.'

'Sure, Dad.'

Audrey was ready and waiting outside the front gate of her house. He suggested that they walk into town rather than get the bus, it being so sunny. Audrey agreed, not suspecting that Dylan was just trying to delay their arrival at the bookshop.

They discussed breakfast on the way—what each had had. Audrey had had porridge and honey. Dylan had eaten eggs and soldiers. They argued over what was the best consistency. Dylan liked it quite runny, so it would soak the toast and stick to his lips. Audrey preferred it when the yoke was not far off from solidifying and could be scooped out. They both agreed that they hated it when they accidentally crunched bits of egg shell. Soon they had to talk about what really mattered.

'What exactly are we going to ask Mr Ebenezer? If we

just ask him straight out, do you know anything about alternative realities, he might get suspicious.'

'We could say we're researching a school project.'

'On alternative realities?'

'Oh, I don't know. We'll think of something to say when we're there.'

Dylan wasn't so sure.

They paused outside St George's walk. It was gloomy in there, trapped away from the sunlight that bathed everywhere outside. A sense of foreboding crept over Dylan.

'Come on,' said Audrey, but she paused when she saw Dylan looking so nervous. 'We don't have to do this Dylan. We could try something else.'

Dylan considered it. What were the chances of Mr Ebenezer being anything but just an eccentric old man? And even if Rollo had told him to stay put—what did that mean? It's not like he was going far from home. And he probably shouldn't base all his actions on the advice of a stranger from another reality that he still didn't really know all that much about. It would be good to start doing something himself. He would stop feeling useless. He turned to Audrey.

'No. We should do this. There's nowhere else we can go.'

'Ebenezer's Books' looked much the same as it always did.

'Are you sure it's open?' asked Audrey, taking in the books stacked in the dusty window, past which there was no one to be seen. Dylan pointed towards the 'open' sign on the door

'Come on then,' he said pushing it open and making the bell tinkle.

Mr Ebenezer was coming around the corner of one of the book passages, heading towards his desk. At first, he only noticed Dylan. To Dylan's surprise, he was smiling warmly.

'Master Thompson,' he started, but stopped when he saw Audrey. For the tiniest fraction of a second, the horrible look he had given him in the street flashed across his face. Dylan noticed Audrey step a little closer to him. He didn't blame her.

'Ah, you have brought a friend with you. What a delightful surprise,' Mr Ebenezer said in an overenthusiastic tone, rubbing his hands on his jacket pocket. 'And what might your name be?'

'Audrey,' she said standing a little apart from Dylan again, trying not to show her uneasiness.

'A pleasure to meet you, Miss Audrey. Let me assure you that any friend of young Dylan here is a friend of mine.' Without waiting for a response, he returned his gaze to Dylan. 'So, you must be back to look for your book again, hmm? Well, I'm afraid I'm going to be leaving the shop in a moment to carry out some errands and won't be needing assistance today.'

'That's ok,' said Dylan. 'I mean we didn't come in to look for the book. We actually came to ask a question. About something else. It's not to do with books.'

'Really? How intriguing. You have a question that's not to do with books, so you make a point of putting it to a book seller. Curious.'

'It's for a school project,' said Audrey. 'On local history.'

'I see.'

'Yes. Dylan thought you might know some interesting things about Croydon.'

'Well, he's certainly right there. I know some very interesting things. So, Dylan, what would you like to ask me?'

Dylan thought he would stumble at this point, but to his surprise, the question came with ease.

'We were wondering if you knew of any strange places in Croydon, or places where strange things happened. We were thinking if we found out something a bit out of the ordinary, we might get more marks for the effort of digging out something less known.'

'Ah, now that does make sense. Right. Something strange, eh? Oh, yes, there have been some strange things happening in Croydon over the years. Most unusual happenings indeed. In unusual places! Now, which one would interest you?'

He stared up at the ceiling and put a hand to his chin, with a look of great concentration. Dylan and Audrey exchanged anxious glances.

'Aha!' he said suddenly. 'I've got it! I'll tell you about the well.'

'The well? What well? There are no wells in Croydon,' Audrey said.

'Aren't there? I can see that as you're so hasty to cut in, maybe you're the sort who wouldn't take the time to notice. Dylan, now, you strike me as the sort to stand back and observe your surroundings in a little more detail. Do you know if there are any wells in Croydon?'

Dylan searched his memory.

'See,' said Audrey. 'Dylan hasn't seen any wells either.'

'Do you mean the wishing well? In the park?' Dylan asked.

Mr Ebenezer smiled widely.

'You see!' He raised a finger at Audrey.

'Hmm, which park then?' Audrey quite obviously didn't want to trust this strange bookseller.

'Why, that would be Haling Grove, would it not, Dylan?'

'Is that right?' Audrey asked Dylan. 'I've never seen it.'

Dylan nodded. 'Yes. It's through the passageway from the fish pond. It's quite tucked away.'

Audrey still looked doubtful, but kept quiet.

'Now, if I may continue. You wanted to know about strange places and strange things? The well is a most peculiar place, where the oddest things have happened. It's not common knowledge, but there used to be a real well there a long, long time ago. Croydon didn't exist back then. There was only a small village, to which the well belonged. Right from as far back as anyone could remember, it was a strange place. People who had been to draw water would return to their families with tales of faeries and pixies that they had seen running around the bottom of the well, swimming in the bucket and generally getting up to mischief. No one minded this really —it was considered quite an entertainment. But after some time people started to become afraid of the well. The faeries and pixies mysteriously vanished. No one saw them any more. Instead there was something else at the well. People didn't often speak of it, because no one knew what it really was, and it unnerved them. They wouldn't see anything when they went to the well, but as they drew the water up, they felt there was a presence down there, something conscious down at the bottom. Some silent, menacing creature lurking and waiting. They said they felt as if it were staring up at them, considering what harm it could do to them. As it was the only well in the village, people didn't stop using it. And they tried to tell themselves they were being foolish —there couldn't be anything alive down there.

One day a boy went to the well to fetch water and never came back. The villagers thought that, even though it was out of character for the boy, he must have run off. But then the baker's daughter went missing the following week when she went to get water. Then the baker himself vanished having gone to the well to look for her. Three more people vanished at the well soon after. Eventually, they decided to fill the well in and trap whatever evil was lurking down there. No one vanished again from that spot. Though, from then on, the ghosts of those that had gone were often sighted wandering aimlessly around the area, occasionally stopping to stare at the spot where the well had been with a look of terror in their eyes. Reports of these sightings can be traced up until the 1930s when the wishing well that is there now was built.

It was a complete coincidence. No one knew there had been a well there. Then one day, in 1934, on a glorious summer's day, there were many families in the park. A young lady of twenty-three years, Miss Gladys Edmondson, was leaning against the well as her family sat on the grass nearby. All of a sudden, she screamed. Some invisible force was dragging her into the well. What it was, nobody knew. The witness reports mention some kind of 'force' or 'presence'. Of course, everyone rushed to the well to pull her out, but there was nothing there at all. Neither Gladys nor anything else. As you will know, Dylan, the well is not even two metres deep. It's purely ornamental. No one knows what happened to poor Gladys Edmondson. It was inexplicable. And nothing out of the ordinary has happened there since.'

Mr Ebenezer was finished.

'Will that do?' he said looking at both of them.

Audrey remained silent.

'Yes. That was exactly what we wanted. Thank you,' said Dylan feeling a little spooked.

'Excellent!' Mr Ebenezer clapped his hands together. 'So glad to be of assistance to you. As I said earlier, I do need to be off. But I shall find you something before you go.'

Mr Ebenezer abruptly shot off to another part of the shop.

'Got it!' he said, thrusting a book into Dylan's hands. '*The Well of Haling Grove—Presences and Vanishings by Tobias Glimshaw.*' Consider it a loan. I'm sure it will prove useful in writing your project. Why don't you take it with you and go to have a look at the well, eh?'

Dylan and Audrey thanked Mr Ebenezer and left the shop with the feeling that he was watching them, even when they were out of sight.

Dylan had seen that well any number of times and never felt there was anything at all peculiar about it. He had even stood inside it. It was only about a metre and a half deep.

They had a look at the book that Mr Ebenezer had placed in his hand earlier that day. It was old and dusty like most of the books in that shop, but it wasn't too scruffy. It didn't feel well read. He had a quick look at the first few pages. It was basically what Mr Ebenezer had told them about the well and the goings on there earlier in the day. He flicked ahead. The text stopped after forty-three pages. The remaining one hundred and fifty or so were blank. Must have been an error at the printers or maybe the book had never been finished.

8

'WHERE IS IT then? I can't see a wishing well,' said Audrey.

'I told you, it's a bit hidden away. Follow me.'

Dylan led Audrey along a pathway through the hedge which led around a large wooden shelter, under a stone archway, to a small area containing a fish pond.

'It's round there,' he said, pointing to an entrance in the wall that looked more like a gap that was there because the builders had run out of bricks. Audrey, however, had walked up to the fish pond and was peering into it.

'Frogspawn!' she said.

Dylan came up beside her and looked down into the water. There was indeed frogspawn. Loads of it.

'But it's the wrong time of year, isn't it?'

'Yeah. How bizarre. Maybe this *is* a weird place.'

'There's probably some explanation for it. We could ask Mr Williams about it. He might be able explain it.'

Mr Williams was one of the science teachers at the school. Audrey looked at Dylan in a funny way. 'After the things you've seen recently?'

'Not everything has to be inexplicable,' said Dylan, shrugging his shoulders. 'But come on, let's have a look at this well.'

They left the pond and went through the entrance in the wall. The well was immediately in front of them. There was no one else around. It looked the same as ever to Dylan. He didn't get any unusual feelings at all. It was just an ordinary wishing well. They walked up to it and looked at it. There was graffiti inside—things like 'Lisa for George', 'Ryan smells of poo' and lots of rude words. The beam across its small roof was riddled with woodworm. Dylan ran his fingers across the holes.

'Disappointing, huh?'

Audrey nodded. 'It is. I was hoping to experience a bit of this weirdness that you've been going through. It's a little dull really.' She hitched herself up and sat on the edge of the well.

Dylan walked off a few steps. He pulled Mr Ebenezer's book out from his bag and began flicking through it. As he flicked through the blank pages, he caught a glimpse of what looked like a picture of the wishing well. He was sure that it hadn't been there before. He tried to find the page again, but he couldn't. He flicked the pages again, like a flick book, back and forth. After doing it a few times, he saw the picture again, but in a different part of the book. Then it vanished. He carried on flicking the pages back and forth. The more he did it, the more he saw the picture. He kept going and eventually the picture was almost constantly visible. It looked like an old animation. Suddenly, he saw there was a girl in the picture, sitting on the edge of the well. Then a shadowy figure rose up, looming behind the girl, as if standing in the well. His arms were raised as if to grab her. The pins and needles sensation shot from the book up his arm and all over him.

'Dylan! Stop that! You did it, you idiot!'

Rollo's voice was coming from behind him. Dylan dropped the book at once. Audrey was staring astonished at something beyond him. He presumed it was Rollo, but he didn't turn round to look. He ran towards her. He couldn't see anything behind her, but he felt a menacing presence there—the shadowy figure from the picture. Before he could get to her, Audrey let out a shocked scream and tumbled backwards as if dragged inside the well. When Dylan got there, he looked inside but she wasn't there. She wasn't anywhere at all. Just behind him was Rollo.

'Where in Vrksnicks did you get that book?'

'Never mind! Where's Audrey?' Dylan circled the well looking for a sign of her.

'It looks, Dylan, like RTH-0709 might not be as untapped as I thought. I'd hazard a guess that there's some kind of doorway to your reality here, in this very spot. And you just opened it up and let your friend be taken through it. *Really.*'

'How could I have opened it? I don't know anything about it.'

Dylan put his hands on his head in frustration.

'The book, the book! Whatever you were doing with it, that's what opened it. It's some kind of key. You seemed to have temporarily unlocked the door.'

Rollo walked back to where Dylan had dropped the book and stooped to pick it up.

'Unlock it again then! We need to get her back.'

Dylan couldn't think straight. Why had he kept trying to find the picture? Why hadn't he told her to get away from the well? He couldn't leave her. He had to find her, wherever she had ended up.

'Calm yourself down. Being panicky won't bring her back. It doesn't always pay to be hasty when dealing with the unknown. Though there is of course a time for haste. It's a matter of judgement. You get a feel for when it's a time to be hasty and when it's a time not to be. Something's telling me not to rush this.'

Dylan breathed deeply and tried to calm down. He was pretty sure that Rollo would be his only hope in getting Audrey back.

'First of all, I'd really like to know where you got this book.' Rollo handled it, looking the cover over but not opening it.

'Mr Ebenezer. He's a weird old man who owns a bookshop in town. He told us about the well. How people vanished here in the past. He gave us a book to take with us.'

'Hmm. What's he like, this Mr Ebenwotsit? Is he a friendly sort of chap?'

'No. Well, I think he pretends to be. He's all like smiley and cheerful, but then he gives you these weird looks sometimes. Kind of... hateful. And he snaps. He got really angry suddenly one time...'

'Not really the sort of person whose advice you should be taking, by the sounds of it, eh? A strange and possibly twisted man tells you about a place where bad things have happened and you just wander off to find it? Doesn't sound sensible, does it?'

'It's not like that. We were asking about places where weird things happened. We wanted to try and investigate for ourselves whatever is going on. And he was the only person we could think of who might have a clue. He might tell us something, some secret without knowing. We didn't tell him why we wanted to know. Not the real reason. Though we weren't completely sure what we were looking for.'

'At least you didn't tell him anything. I'm going to look this man up. Sounds like there's something wrong about him. But I guess we should try and rescue this friend of yours first.'

Dylan nodded. His stomach fell as he thought of Audrey. He couldn't imagine what she might be going through, and it was all his fault. Rollo opened the book with his long fingers and flicked through the pages. He handed it back to Dylan.

'Now, show me what you did to open the gateway. Let's see if we can get ourselves to wherever they went.' He looked over Dylan's shoulder as Dylan started flicking the pages back and forth as he had before.

'Last time a picture appeared. Of the well. And suddenly Audrey was in it and some sort of shadow thing turned up behind her.' He carried on flicking the pages but nothing happened. The blank pages remained blank.

'It doesn't look like it's working now, whatever you did,' said Rollo. 'Maybe it's because whatever came out of the well got Audrey and doesn't have the urge to come back just yet.'

Rollo took the book from Dylan and walked toward the well. Dylan followed close behind. Rollo tore a page out of the book.

'You can't do that! Mr Ebenezer will go spare!'

'I don't really care if he does,' said Rollo, tearing out a few more pages.

'What are you doing anyway?'

'It's quite often with these sorts of locks that if the key stops existing, the lock gives up on existing too.'

Rollo tore out a whole handful of pages. On the next go, he tore the spine of the book in half. A throbbing hum filled the air around them. It was emanating from the well. The hairs on Dylan's neck stood on end.

'I think that's done it,' said Rollo. 'Come on. Let's go get her. No dilly dallying.' Rollo climbed into the well without looking back and appeared to slip out of existence.

Dylan looked around him. There was no one there. He shrugged his shoulders—he had no choice—and jumped into the well. He fell into a darkness much like before when Rollo had taken him away, but it only lasted an instant this time.

The next moment he was in a darkened room. As his eyes adjusted, he could just make out two large windows at the far side. A tiny amount of moonlight came through. Looking around, he could see strange shadows all over the place filling the darkness, but he couldn't make out what anything was.

There was a sudden noise of something toppling over.

'Drat,' said Rollo fumbling around until a light shone in his hand. He appeared to be holding a glowing egg. There still wasn't much light to see by, but Dylan could make out a large table in the middle of the room, at which Rollo was rooting around.

'Aha,' he said, 'here's a match.' He lit a couple of candles on the table and passed one to Dylan. 'Let's have a look around, eh?'

They appeared to be in a room in quite an ancient and grand house. Victorian looking. It was extraordinarily cluttered. There were dressers and shelves taking up most of the wall space. Every surface in the room was overcrowded with all manner of things. There were thimbles, ornamental gnomes, people and faeries, drawing pins, coins, curtain hooks, finger traps, broken piano keys —possibly from the piano a few metres away, barely visible under the things heaped on top of it—all kinds of boxes, jewellery, food tins, dice, pieces from board games, knives, jigsaw pieces, buttons, swords, even a suit of armour propped against a wall.

He made his way over to the windows, almost tripping over a rocking horse which was wearing a pirate hat. Rollo was attempting to open one of the windows without much luck. Dylan peered out of the other. He looked up and saw the moon, shining palely in the sky. It was full. Thousands of stars littered the darkness. Dylan had never seen so many, and not so clear. He looked down. Down, there was nothing. Just darkness. No stars. He shivered. Where were they? Was the house floating?

'Rollo, what are we going to do once you've got the window open? There doesn't appear to be anything to land on, if we climb out.'

'I hadn't thought that far ahead yet. But there doesn't appear to be any other way out of here.'

Dylan walked around the edges of the room, leaving Rollo wrestling with the window. There really didn't appear to be any doors, of any sort. If there was anything like a trapdoor in the floor, it would take an age to find, with everything strewn everywhere.

Something on a dresser caught his eye. It was a decorative plate featuring a circular pattern in the centre of which was a navy blue owl. He held the candle closer to get a better look. As he did so, the owl blinked. Must have been a trick of the light, he thought. He stared at the owl to see if it would happen again. Nothing happened at first. He was about to look away when the owl looked from side to side, as if to see if anyone was watching. Then it winked at Dylan. Dylan winked back. The owl replied with a wink. Dylan smiled. With a flutter, the little owl flew out of the plate, straight across the room and through a door that had definitely not been there a moment ago.

A faint 'twit-twooo' sounded from wherever it had flown to outside. Without thinking, Dylan followed it. Beyond the door was a short corridor ending in some wooden steps winding upwards. He could just see the little owl sitting on the first step, as if waiting for him. He moved towards the stairs. As soon as he got there, the owl flew up a few more steps, impatiently hopping from foot to foot as Dylan began to ascend the stairs. He was climbing carefully, with only the candlelight to guide him. On the walls he noticed paintings of very serious people who seemed to be staring at him. It made him shiver. It must be a trick of the light, he kept telling himself. Eventually, he reached the top. There were three doorways in front of him. The owl excitedly flew through the one on the left. Dylan followed.

He entered a huge attic room with a slanting ceiling. More light from the moon and stars was able to enter than in the room he had come from because of a huge floor to ceiling window. The place was bare, apart from an enormous bed in front of the window. A strange frame with canvas wings stretching over its sides was suspended above it, making it look like a four poster bed. The owl was jumping up and down at the foot of it.

'Well done on finding that door.' Rollo's voice was coming from behind him. 'Couldn't get those blasted windows to budge downstairs. This looks promising. Looks like this little fellow thinks we should take the bed outside.'

The owl was now jumping up and down on one of the window's handles, as if trying to open it. Rollo obliged and turned the handle. This window opened without a problem. A breeze entered the room in a gentle rush. The wings above the bed rippled slightly. The owl flew out of the window and fluttered about waiting for them.

'Come on then, Dylan, let's both give this bed a big push and jump on it as soon as it's outside the window.'

Rollo was pushing hard against the end of the bed. 'What's keeping you?'

'Is it safe? Where are we going?'

'Who knows? But this little owl chap seems like a good bet and I can't think of anything else to do. Can't see any sign of Audrey here, wherever here is.'

Dylan couldn't argue with that. He knelt down and put his shoulders to the frame. Rollo counted to three and they pushed the bed with all their might into the night air, quickly leaping onto it. Dylan's heart jumped. His head swam as he contemplated the void below. He scrambled to the middle of the bed. The owl danced excitedly in front of them as the bed gracefully glided forward under the the moon and the stars.

The bed felt surprisingly safe. It was large and sturdy and showed no sign of tipping over. Parts of it creaked but it felt reassuring rather than worrying. Dylan actually felt a sort of calmness as the wind ruffled his hair.

The owl flew in a straight line for a long time and it didn't occur to Dylan or Rollo that they might need to turn at some point, or how exactly to do so. Suddenly the owl flew down and to the left.

'Quick, lean against the posts,' shouted Rollo, who had leapt up and was leaning into a post at the front left of the bed. Dylan edged towards the back left post without standing up. Shaking slightly, he grabbed hold of the post tightly and pulled himself up. With all their weight on the left side, the bed slowly started to spiral downwards anti-clockwise in a wide arc, following the owl.

Dylan stared down into the darkness, trying not to lose concentration on holding on. If he lost his grip, he would fall. There was not telling how far. Presumably there was a bottom somewhere. But maybe there wasn't, and he'd be left falling forever. Neither proposition was attractive.

It felt like they were slowly descending for hours, always following the owl. Dylan's arms were aching by the time he finally saw something looming out of the darkness. It was hard to make out at first—nothing more than a grey speck. As they gradually got closer, Dylan was able to see what it was.

'A castle!'

Rollo didn't reply. Soon Dylan was able to make out more detail. It was a large building, floating in the air as the house they had flown from had been. The castle had no courtyard. In the middle of a roof, slanted on all sides, was a big round dome with a slit in the middle; an observatory, Dylan soon worked out. There were turrets along the castle walls, with slightly fatter and taller ones on each of the four corners. Apart from the fact that it was floating in the middle of nowhere, it wouldn't have looked to out of place in his own reality. He had expected things to be very alien in these other places, more incomprehensible. So far, things seemed to be variants of each other. But then again he had only seen very little. They were almost level with the castle.

'Er, Rollo?'

'Yes?' His voice was calm.

'I think we're going to smash into the wall of the castle.'

Immediately in front of them was a blank wall of stone. Further down was a window—a huge one made of stained glass. Flickering light was shining out from the inside, lighting up its abstract and colourful patterns.

'I was thinking that too,' said Rollo, a bit too calmly.

'So, erm, do we have a plan?'

'I reckon we sit on the front of the bed to try and get it to head for the window. And pull the covers over our heads.'

'Why pull the covers over our heads? We won't be able to see where we're going!'

'That's right. But we'll be less likely to cut ourselves to ribbons when we go through the glass. And if we don't make the window... well, it'll be too late by then anyway. This way we'll be in less of a panic.'

Carefully, they manoeuvred down to the front of the bed. As they did so, the bed dipped forward and changed its trajectory. It looked like they were on course to collide with the window. The owl had now settled on the railing at the front, facing forward like a tiny figurehead.

'See you on the other side, Dylan. Hold on tight,' said

Rollo as they pulled the duvet over their heads. Dylan held on to the bedstead as tight as he could through the feathery cushioning of the duvet and closed his eyes. It was an odd sensation. He hadn't ever thought he would end up sitting in bed with the covers over his head, while gliding through the air, hoping to crash through the window of a castle, suspended in the middle of nowhere. It's funny how things turn out, he was thinking, just as there was a huge crash, followed by the tinkling of raining glass and a lurch as the bed fell and then skidded across something solid, before crashing into something even more solid and flinging Dylan and Rollo into the unknown.

9

DYLAN FOUND HIMSELF a little bruised and shaken after being flung from the bed, but he wasn't too worse for wear. He still seemed to be in one piece. He dusted himself off and stood up. A few feet away, Rollo was doing the same. They were in a large room with a very high ceiling, illuminated chiefly by a big fire blazing in the middle of the room and there were torches all along the many pillars that lined the walls. There were many doors, all ornately decorated. The stained glass window they had crashed though was almost obliterated, most of it being spread out across the floor. The bed had collapsed and the wings had great tears running down them. Dylan couldn't see anyone in the room except Rollo, but it felt like there was someone else there. He strained his eyes and searched the place. He couldn't see anyone, but there were plenty of nooks and crannies that someone could be hiding in. The only sound other than the crackle of the fire was a grandfather clock that was ticking nearby. The ticking was irregular. It would tick and tock as normal, but every now and then it would pause or speed up. Dylan watched the pendulum with fascination. It seemed to have a will of its own. He noticed that the hours were in the wrong order too.

'What now?' Dylan whispered. He still felt like someone else was there with them.

'We'll have a word with whoever is here.' Rollo kept his voice low, too. 'And take it from there.'

He strode confidently towards the centre of the room. Dylan followed, not wanting to be left on his own.

'Salutations,' said Rollo. 'Salutations to whoever may or may not be in this room, and may or may not be the keeper of this castle. And apologies for destroying such fine stained glass. I'm afraid it was rather unavoidable. It's always a shame when great art goes to waste, but when it's a choice between you and the art, it's a pretty easy one to make, hmm?'

He let his words hang in the air, waiting for a response. Dylan thought he could hear a harpsichord or some such instrument in the distance, in a far off room. When he strained to catch it, it went silent and he couldn't be sure if he had heard it or not.

'Anyone at home?' asked Rollo loudly, walking round the fire in the middle of the room casually. 'They won't mind if we take a look around then, eh, Dylan?'

Suddenly, as if in response to his words, the fire roared up so high that it gave the impression that it was straining to touch the ceiling. It made Dylan jump, but Rollo laughed. 'Got something to hide, do we?'

Dylan noticed something unusual in the huge shadows of the flickering flames cast on the wall and floor in front of him. One of the shadows didn't seem to be flickering so much as moving purposefully around the edge of the fire. It was hard to spot at first, among the normal shadows, but once you caught track of it, you could sense purpose in its movement. The shadow disentangled itself from the rest and slowly started to reach out towards Dylan and Rollo.

Dylan tugged Rollo's coat sleeve and pointed at it. They watched as the shadow became a thin, long shape across the floor. It rose before their eyes, expanding into three dimensions like a balloon being inflated, turning into a rather short man with dark eyeballs and burning red pupils. He was bald on top with slightly long hair around the sides. He wore a navy blue cloak over a green tunic and dark trousers. He stared at them in silence.

'Ah, well, it seems that someone was home after all. How do you do?' Rollo bowed. 'My name is Rollovkarghjiczni-legogh-Vylpophyngh, and this here is my young friend, Dylan. I apologise again for our unorthodox entrance. Would you be able to tell us who owns this castle?'

The man's eyes narrowed. 'How did you get here?' he said. His voice was raspy, as if he had some bees in his throat. He looked at them with no expression.

'Through a wishing well,' said Rollo.

'A wishing well?'

'Yes, a wishing well. In a completely different reality. And, of course, we had to fly the bed down to the castle once we had got here.'

'Impossible!'

'I wouldn't say impossible, would you Dylan? Not when it's already happened.'

The man scowled at Rollo and took a few paces. Then he looked at them opening his mouth as if to say something.

They waited for him to speak. Silence.

'So, now we've established how we arrived, would you be able to tell me who owns this castle? I have some questions that I want to ask.'

'No one owns the castle.'

'Oh, do you share it with others? Is it like a squat?'

'There are no others.' The man, who remained nameless, wasn't giving much away.

'In the castle?'

'Here. Anywhere here. No other intelligent beings, anyway,' he said, looking at the owl which had flown down from somewhere and was perching on Dylan's shoulder.

'So which reality is this? Nothing rings a bell. Is it untapped? I mean, in a known way? Surely, I'd know about it, if it was. And how come it's linked to RTH-0709 when nowhere else is?'

'This place isn't anyone's business.'

'Isn't it? I think it is. Our friend was pulled from his reality into this one by a creature, some kind of being. And if you're the only one here, one would have to assume that it was you, don't you think? I think the kidnapping of our friend makes this place very much our business, don't you agree?'

Silence.

'Well, you're not denying it,' stated Rollo.

The man scowled and started to walk away.

Rollo and Dylan followed him. He led them up a dark spiral staircase, dimly lit by candles that were few and far between. He was muttering to himself as he went along.

'Untapped, what are they talking about... no privacy... shouldn't have got hungry, shouldn't have left the well shut...'

They kept walking upwards for a very long time. Dylan didn't dare ask where they were going. The strange little man might be leading them towards Audrey. They passed many closed doors of different shapes and colours, all looking firmly shut. He wondered what was behind them. They gave off a sinister air.

His legs started to ache. Surely the castle wasn't this high? They must have gone up at least twenty floors. Dylan's right leg suddenly cramped and he had to stop for a moment. The others carried on without him. He'd soon catch up when the cramp had gone.

As the others moved on, the dim light from the candles began to fade. They weren't just fading, the shadows were creeping forward and covering the light. They were reaching for him. His cramp had gone, but he was rooted to the spot. He tried to move his legs, but they felt like metal on a highly strong magnet. The shadows drew closer, reaching around the outside wall. He stared in horror as they almost touched him.

A firm hand clasped his shoulder, making him jump. The shadows retreated.

'What are you doing!' The angry voice of the little man rasped in his ear. He must have realised and come back to find him. 'Don't get left behind. The castle will hide you and you will never be found. Hurry up.'

Eventually they reached what appeared to be the top of the castle. Facing them was a large landing with a huge bolted wooden door that looked like it was designed for keeping out invading hordes. Or keep whatever was on the other side in. The bolts were on their side.

The stranger was still acting as if Rollo and Dylan were not there. He walked to the corner where he picked up a small set of wooden steps. He carried it over to the door and set it down next to the bolts, climbing up and undoing them. After he had climbed back down, he moved to open the door. It looked like he'd never be able to shift it on his own.

'Do you need some help with that?' Dylan asked.

The man turned and gave Dylan a contemptuous look. Without turning back, he gave the door a slight push with one hand. The door swung open easily as if it were as light as balsa wood.

'Follow me,' said the stranger walking into the room beyond. Dylan looked at Rollo, who shrugged his shoulders as if to say that they might as well.

The room turned out to be the observatory that Dylan had spotted from outside the castle. It was very wide. Only the centre was illuminated from the light of the stars, through a slit running the whole way across the middle of the domed ceiling. Protruding through the gap was the silhouette of a massive telescope whose base was in the centre of the room where the stranger was waiting for them.

'Your friend is here.'

'Where?' asked Dylan, looking round. The room was too dark around the edges to make out anything.

'You will know soon enough. I will let her return to you. But I must show you something first. And then you must promise me something.'

He stood on a step at the base of the telescope and put an eye to the sight. He pulled a lever and the telescope swooped round to the left and would have knocked Dylan and Rollo over, if they hadn't managed to duck in time. It clunked to a standstill. He pulled two other handles on either side. The telescope moved tiny amounts as he adjusted them.

'There it is! You—look at this, look at this.' He was gesturing frantically.

Dylan put the sight to his eye. All he could see was the night sky full of stars. He strained to perceive anything else, but couldn't work out what it was, he wanted him to see.

'There isn't anything unusual,' said Dylan, 'Just the sky and stars.'

'Look harder, look harder! Don't you see it?'

Dylan looked back into the telescope. He couldn't see anything strange. As he continued to stare, he began to sense that there was something weird in what he was seeing, but he couldn't put his finger on it.

'I can't quite see…' he started, but suddenly he realized what it was.

'The stars are going out! It's like they're being swallowed.'

One by one, stars were indeed stopping to show light, as if they had never been there in the first place. They were rising from the top right of Dylan's vision in an expanding line, blending into a darkness pushing outward. Dylan shivered. It didn't seem right at all.

'Let me have a look, Dylan,' Rollo said urgently.

Rollo bent his head to the telescope.

Dylan watched with curiosity. He still wondered at Rollo's lack of facial features. Rollo moved the sight in a position that suggested his eyes were roughly in the same place as a human's, but his face hovered a few inches from the lens.

He was silent for a couple of minutes.

'This is very bad news. Very bad news indeed.' He turned his face to the little man. 'It looks like your reality is unravelling.'

'It's being consumed! It's been wearing down at the edges and *it* has broken through.'

Dylan shuddered to think what *it* might be.

'It's getting stronger. And faster!'

'Why is it consuming this reality?'

'No time! We must escape. It will take us—it will reduce us to nothing. It is eating all reality.'

'But what is it? Can't we stop it?'

'Stop it? No, we cannot stop the Deadly Dimension.'

'Deadly Dimension?'

'We must escape!' The little man looked through the telescope and then frantically motioned for Rollo to look. He did so and then motioned for Dylan to look. The darkness had covered a much greater area than it had before. Now it was unmistakable that it was like a curtain being hastily drawn across the stars with increasing speed.

'I'll give you your friend back. But you must promise

to help me to escape.'

Rollo put his hands on his hips. 'I can see that we don't have much time to argue, but you do realize there's no guarantee how long you will survive if we take you back to this boy's reality? No one has ever been able to settle permanently outside their own.'

'Don't put him off, we need Audrey!' hissed Dylan, wondering where Rollo's interests might lie.

'If I don't come with you, I will cease to exist as soon as the Deadly Dimension gets here!' shouted the stranger, raising his hands desperately in the air and ignoring Dylan.

'Fine. We'll take you with us if you give us back Audrey. Agreed, Dylan?'

Dylan nodded, wondering whether there would be time. They should be getting on to escape that Deadly Dimension.

'Okay. We promise to take you with us—now give us back Audrey at once!'

'Yes, yes, I'll give her back.'

The stranger walked over to another bank of levers, a few paces away from the telescope, and started pulling at various ones. Suddenly, light bathed the room as hundreds of lamps dangling down from the dome lit up. Around the perimeter of the room was an unbroken row of rectangular wooden boxes, about seven foot tall. There was a creaking noise and a mechanical hand attached to a long metal arm descended from a hole in the ceiling. As he pulled the levers, it swung round, reaching out towards the boxes. It hovered above a section before lowering and clasping one. Dylan guessed that Audrey must be inside. Both anger and fear rose in him. He hoped she wasn't hurt—she had better not be hurt! The mechanical hand had the box firmly in its grasp. It rose again, lifting the box. There was another loud creak, the arm swung back precariously to the middle of the room.

'Careful!' exclaimed Dylan.

The little man gave Dylan a hateful look, but didn't say anything. The box was lowered down in front of them. As soon as it touched the floor, the hand let go and retracted back into the ceiling.

'Here she is, here she is.' The stranger walked up to the box and began fiddling with a huge ring of keys that he lifted from his belt. After finding a particular one, he put the key to a padlock attached to the lid of the box and unlocked it. He threw the it open. Inside was Audrey, nestled in straw, her eyes closed and not moving. She was pale and did not seem to be breathing.

'Audrey!' shouted Dylan. 'What have you done to her?'

'Calm down! She's just asleep. More or less. I will revive her.'

The stranger looked up at Audrey's face. He took hold of either side of the box and held his breath until he was red in the face. He stayed like that a few moments and then suddenly started to vibrate. Dylan could feel the vibration through the floor. It increased in rate and a hum filled the air. Suddenly, the humming stopped and the stranger shouted with all his might:

'WAKE UP!'

Audrey's eyes flicked open. She looked at him, then at Rollo. Finally, she looked at Dylan. Her brow furrowed in confusion.

'What's going on?' she asked.

Dylan was going to answer, but Rollo beat him to it.

'That horrible man pulled you through the well in the park and into his own reality. I don't know why he put you in a box. There's something called the Deadly Dimension—it's about to swallow us all up and out of existence! We've agreed to help your kidnapper escape in exchange for your return.'

Perplexed, Audrey looked at him, but before he could say any more, a loud thrum filled the air. That pins and needles sensation took over Dylan's body with greater intensity than he had ever felt before.

10

'IT'S GETTING CLOSER!'

They all looked at Dylan.

'What is?' asked Audrey stepping out of the box, brushing straw off herself.

'The Deadly Dimension. I can feel it.'

Rollo turned to the stranger and whispered urgently. 'How did *you* get through to their reality? Will we have to go back the same way we came?'

'There is a pathway, another well. But I cannot open it so soon. It weakens me.'

'Let's head that way anyway,' shouted Rollo. 'As I'm the only one here who can slip, it looks like it's going to be up to me to get us out of here. It'll probably be easier to slip where the barrier between realities is weakened. Let's act, not panic.'

Without saying a word, the strange little man scampered off. They followed as quickly as they could. Before leaving the room, Dylan looked back at the boxes lined up against the walls and shivered. If Audrey had been in one of them, were there more people in the others? He thought about the tales of the people who had gone missing in the park.

Instead of going back down the winding stares, the little man let out a shrill whistle. The stones in the wall slid grindingly to one side revealing an entrance into a square chamber. They entered and the stones slid back in place. They were in total darkness.

'Down!' shouted the man. 'Fast!'

The whole room started to plummet quickly. It was a lift! And not one that felt very safe. 'Why didn't we use the lift when we came up?' Dylan asked as his stomach lurched.

'Secrets!' shouted the little man.

They descended for a few minutes. At the speed they were going, they must have been much further down from where Dylan and Rollo had entered the castle.

'Hold on to the rails!'

As they groped in the dark to find the rails, the lift gradually slowed down, but it was still going at a fair pace when it suddenly stopped. If they hadn't been holding on to something, they would have all been in a pile in the middle of the floor.

The stones in the wall slipped aside revealing an ornate door. The stranger fiddled with his keys and unlocked it. A long dark corridor loomed in front of them. As they moved along it, candles ignited on the walls nearby, going out as they went past. A slight tingle went down Dylan's spine.

'Are you OK?' he whispered to Audrey,

'I think so,' she whispered back. 'I mean I don't remember much. I remember being pulled into the well and feeling pretty weird, and then that horrible little man shouting 'wake up' in my face.'

'So, I guess you believe me now? This isn't all in my head.'

'It's certainly strange. Is that… man with the egg for a head Rollo? I'm starting to think that all you told me is real.'

'Starting to?' groaned Dylan. 'You're in a different reality, following someone who looks like he's made of bone and a little man with glowing red eyes!'

Audrey frowned but didn't say anything. They kept on down the corridor at a fast pace. When would they reach their destination?

The corridor wasn't ending any time soon. Dylan felt a pressure pushing him. It made his head feel heavy, as if he was about to fall asleep. He tried to ignore it, forcing himself to move faster. Audrey struggled to keep pace. Pins and needles crept up Dylan's legs.

'Run!' he shouted urgently. They all started to race down the corridor. A solid thrum was vibrating through the walls pounding the air. Dylan saw Rollo look backwards as he ran and then run even faster. Dylan risked a glance behind him. In the distance he could see nothing at all. It wasn't darkness, it was just nothing. The space was becoming null and void. He dared not look any more. Everything behind them was ceasing to exist at a very fast rate. Soon they wouldn't exist either.

The end of the corridor came into view. There was no door, the stones just opened up revealing a small round room, at the centre of which was a tiny well. Dylan's heart was thumping like a hammer.

'What now?' shouted Audrey. Her voice was almost lost in the vibrations in the air.

'Everyone! Hold hands around the well!' ordered Rollo at the top of his voice.

They did as he said. They could see the corridor being quickly being erased, as if it had never existed. This must be happening all around them. The edges of the Deadly Dimension were nearly on them. Audrey screamed.

'Silence!' shouted Rollo urgently. 'I have to concentrate. It's highly dangerous to slip more than two people at a time and I want to make sure we don't lose any parts o…ur… b…die…as w…'

Rollo's words seemed to be disappearing into that dark void, sucked out of existence. Dylan looked around wide eyed. The walls of the room were gone. They were standing around the well and that was all that existed. Beyond them everything was dark and he could no longer feel the hands of the others.

'It's got us!' he thought frantically. 'Everything is gone. Or is it? I'm here. Otherwise I wouldn't still be thinking. If I'm thinking, I must still exist. This darkness happened when we slipped before. Rollo's done it.'

All of a sudden there was light. All four of them, Dylan, Rollo, Audrey and the little man were holding hands again. But they were in the sky, falling very fast towards the ground below them.

'A bit of a miscalculation!' shouted Rollo above the wind that was whipping their faces. They continued falling. Then there was darkness.

Dylan found himself alone sitting in a field of grass that felt like rubber under a purple sky, criss-crossed with lightning. Before he had time to look round, darkness descended. He felt himself being lifted into the air again and thrown down onto a sandy beach. Light returned. He was lying on his back looking at a clear blue sky. Audrey was lying next to him unconscious. There was no sign at all of Rollo or the little man. He leant over to check she was still breathing. As he did so, a huge wave broke over them and rolled them tumbling up the beach. Audrey spluttered awake. She shook her wet hair and peeled some seaweed off her face.

'Everything went very dark,' she said. 'And then I was in a hot air balloon with a woman who looked a lot like a... a confused tree. And then there was more darkness and then I was on a banana bus, I think. Where are we? There's not usually a beach in Croydon. I'd have noticed. And if there was, it wouldn't be so nice as this.'

Dylan looked around. The beach was more than nice. It was beautiful. The sand was warm and bone white and the sea that had washed over them was the clearest he had ever seen. Behind them was a thick forest. The trees looked normal. He couldn't tell if they were back in their reality or not. If they were, they were far from home.

'The darkness always happens when you slip,' explained Dylan. 'I'm almost getting used to it.' He breathed in the fresh salty air. 'It's definitely not Croydon. It's far too cool. But how on Earth do we get back if we don't know where we are? There's nothing to tell us if we're in our own reality or not. If we're not, I don't know that we could get back without Rollo.'

'Then let's try to find him.' Audrey stood up and dusted off the sand. 'And let's see what's around. There's not much else we can do.'

They started to walk along the shore. Neither of them suggested walking in among the trees. They looked dense. Not menacing, but as if they would swallow you up. It would be too easy to get lost in them and Rollo would be much better able to see them on the shore, if he was around.

Dylan was uneasy. He tried not to show it as Audrey

didn't seem to be put out much at all, as always. The place was ideal and part of him wanted just to explore. But it might not be their reality. What had Rollo said about people spending too long in realities outside their own? Not to mention the Deadly Dimension. Whatever that was, if it turned up, they didn't stand a chance.

They walked along. The beach started to get rocky and rose into high cliffs in the distance. They walked along in silence for a while. As they approached the cliff, Dylan heard an unusual clicking sound coming from some rocks strewn across the beach.

'Can you hear that?'

'Hear what?'

The clicking noises stopped.

'Your mind must have been playing on tricks you,' said Audrey. Dylan didn't reply. Then the clicking started again. He tapped Audrey's shoulder, put a finger up to his lips and pointed to his ears. They continued walking.

As they came closer to the rocks, the sound became louder. They exchanged glances. The sound was becoming intense and seemed awesome and hostile. Dylan wanted to turn and head back to the less rocky part of the beach, but when he looked behind them, he saw that lots of rocks had piled themselves up, as if to block their way. They began to run. The clicking filled the air so much that it almost sounded like rainfall.

They kept going until they came upon a huge boulder that stood in the middle of the sand.

'Halt!' shouted the boulder.

Shocked by the voice, they stopped immediately.

The clicking sound quickly hushed. Dylan and Audrey looked at each other. Maybe they were experiencing some kind of joint auditory hallucination. 'Come on, it's just a rock,' said Dylan moving forwards.

'I just said, *halt!*' the boulder shouted.

Dylan froze.

'Why? Why should we pay attention to a big lump of rock?' Audrey was trying to sound confident, but there was a slight tremor in her voice.

'Rock?! You dare call me a lump of rock! Whatever you creatures are, don't you have any manners?'

There was rumbling as two massive red crab-like pincers emerged from either side of the boulder, followed by legs and then two eyes on long stalks that waved in the air. All around them, the smaller rocks began to sprout into crabs too till they were surrounded by thousands of these creatures.

'What are you?' asked the biggest crab.

It felt funny, a huge rock-like crab asking what *you* are. Then it occurred to him that *they* must be the strangers.

'We're humans,' said Dylan. 'We got here by accident. We're not exactly sure where we are.'

'Humans? Human *beings*? We've been told to watch

out for a 'human being' matching your description by the Intrapelatio Union. But only one. What is this?' The crab extended a pincer in Audrey's direction, causing her to lean back. 'Another human? Are we to be infested?'

'This is my friend, Audrey. It's just the two of us. No one else in our reality has a clue that there are realities other than our own. As least not in this sense.'

'Ha!' said the crab, waving its pincers. 'Yes, the untapped reality. The Intrapelatio tried keeping it quiet, but these things always leak out—big news always does. What egos, to think all existence is yours!'

Dylan suddenly wondered if he had said too much. Rollo would be angry. But he wasn't standing in front of two huge pincers and surrounded by thousands of smaller but still deadly looking ones. He'd keep quiet about the Deadly Dimension, for now.

'How did you get here then? Surely you can't slip if you're from an *un-tapped* reality? Someone brought you here? Someone is aiding you?'

'Our friend Rollo,' said Audrey, 'but he doesn't seem to be here. He helped us escape from the Dead-'

'Shhh!' Dylan cut her off. 'Don't tell them anything.'

'It's hard not to with all these pincers waving about.'

'What are you hiding?' The crab raised its voice. The crowd of smaller crabs started talking all at once. 'What are they hiding?' they asked in a sea of murmur.

'Tell us!' shouted the big crab. 'Tell us, tell us,' echoed

the smaller crabs. They started moving in on Dylan and Audrey. 'Tell us and we won't hurt you,' said the large crab.

'Maybe we should,' Audrey whispered to Dylan. Dylan shook his head.

'You won't hurt us!' he said out loud.

'Won't we?'

'We wouldn't be much use to the Intrapelatio if we're harmed. We're very fragile.'

'Really?'

The crabs were closing in on them. They huddled together holding hands. They didn't stand much chance. Thousands of staring eyes on stalks were waving at them and pincers snapped the air. Soon the crabs were on top of them and as their pincers closed on Dylan and Audrey's legs and arms, everything went black.

We've slipped, thought Dylan. Had Rollo saved them? Or had the crabs taken them somewhere? Suddenly they were out of the darkness, still surrounded by crabs, but not as many. Only a few of the smaller ones and the huge one that had done all the talking.

They were in a rather ordinary looking large hallway, the sort you'd get in the entrance of an office building. He would have thought they were back in their own reality, if it wasn't for small details. There weren't any light bulbs—the light seemed to be there without coming from a particular source. There were two desks in the centre of the room. Computer screens hung in the air unaided like glowing images. Sitting behind one desk, was a man in a suit with the head of a badger, at the other was a woman who looked almost human, except for her hooked beak and spider-like arms, four of which she was using to move something around on the desk.

The large crab told the smaller ones to guard Audrey and Dylan and walked over to the desk to speak to the badger-man and spider-bird-lady. Office workers of all shapes and sizes walked past staring at the two humans with extreme curiosity. Some were wanting to know who they were, but the crabs snapped their pincers and told them to go away.

The large crab returned.

'They wish to see you immediately.'

'Who does?' asked Audrey.

'The Intrapelatio Council! They very interested in meeting you straight away. Follow me.'

They followed the large crab who scuttled off sideways, like crabs do. He led them down a long corridor and into a large round room, coming to a stop in the middle. High up around the edges of the rooms were seats containing a number of different sorts of beings.

'Council,' shouted the crab sounding very official. 'I am Carrfyx of reality Hmmnphrr. I bring before you the human being you have been looking for, alongside another that found its way to Hmmnphrr as well.'

'We thank you, Carrfyx, bzz,' said a large bee that sat in the council. 'But we must ask you to step out of the council chamber for us to question the human beingzzz. This situation is highly confidential.'

'But don't we have a right to know what's going on? There's all sorts of rumours appearing about these humans and their reality. And there's unease at the sudden lack of communication with certain realities being cut off, all since the discovery of this previously un-tapped reality. What was it...RTH-0709?'

'You're not meant to know about that!' grumbled a creature that looked like he was made out of blackcurrant jelly. He struck the desk in front of him and wobbled. 'Those co-ordinates are highly classified!'

'We will have to investigate how this information has leaked, but we have more pressing matters to attend to. Information will be given out to the public of the Intrapelatio, as and when it is deemed suitable. For the moment, please leave us, Carrfyx.'

'Very well, Pilate Gerskin,' said Carrfyx sidling out of the room mumbling to himself under his breath.

The bee type creature, Pilate Gerskin, turned his attention back towards Dylan and Audrey.

'Now,' he continued. 'It izz very interesting that you two beings are from an un-tapped reality, yet one of you at least has been spotted in more than one reality besides your own. How can this be? How did you manage to slip?'

'Well… it's hard to say, exactly,' said Dylan.

'Why? Don't you know how to slip?'

'No.'

'Then someone who does know must have helped you, yezz?'

'No one helped us,' said Audrey. 'It just happened.'

'Impossible!' Commented a fleshy vulture-necked creature. 'No one slips without knowing how!'

'Really, I did,' objected Dylan. 'I started seeing things in our reality. Unusual things. Images of creatures from other realities. And I saw some creatures enter our reality to capture some kind of beast and everything kind of stopped.'

'What did these creatures look like?' asked Pilate Gerskin.

Dylan described the horned creatures that he had seen in Covent Garden on his birthday.

'Slarpups! They have been to RTH-0709! Pilate Vengling, what do you know of this?' Pilate Gerskin pointed across the room at the creature called Vengling. She was one of the slarpups.

'I know nothing of this, Pilate Gerskin. It would have been reported and I would have been notified,' said Pilate Vengling in a very solemn voice.

At this there was a lot of murmuring.

'Quiet, pleazz,' said Pilate Gerskin. 'Pilate Vengling, the slarpups have not always, should we say, proven themselves to be transparent. If there is any chance that your IntraPolice have worked out how to slip to RTH-0709, please inform us now!'

'It is possible that they got there accidentally. But not in the sense that these human beings accidentally slipped. When our police are tracking creatures that are slipping uncontrollably, they catch their scent and are able to skip in their wake without necessarily knowing where they're slipping to. It could be that they followed this beast back to RTH-0709 and back out again without noting their co-ordinates.'

'Hmmm. Pozzible. And I guess it might also be possible that these human beings are not telling the truth. Either way, what they say is worrying. It seems that other realities are bleeding into theirs, as has been reported in a number of realities in the Intrapelatio Union. All thizz started after the sanctuary was closed. And now with communications failing with certain branches of the Union, we must work out what is going on. What izz *happening* in that sanctuary?'

A murmur started again and the noise soon rose into a heated hubbub.

'What do we do?' Audrey said to Dylan. There didn't seem much point in whispering, as no one was paying them any attention any longer.

'Good question,' said Dylan.

'We seem to be increasingly clueless in all this.'

'Well, we've not much to go on. It's all a bit new to us.'

Pins and needles shot through Dylan's body.

'Something's going to happen,' he said.

'Like wha-...' before Audrey could finish a creaking groan filled the air causing the whole room to quieten down. It stopped for a moment and there wasn't a sound. Then it came again, like metal scraping against metal, then suddenly there was a fizzle and a burning smell and with a loud *pop*, Rollo appeared in the middle of the room.

'Dylan, Audrey,' he nodded, 'Pilates. How are we all?'

Pilate Gerskin rose. He was outraged.

'Rollovkarghjicznilegogh-Vylpophyngh! This chamber is meant to be impenetrable! I would very much like to know how you slipped inside it, but I also want to know why you have not reported back to us for five weekz! And why you appear to know these humanzzz!!!!'

'Gersky, has anyone ever told you that you use too many exclamation marks? They really should.'

'Enough! We have always tolerated your foolishness to a degree because of your uses, but you are treading a very thin line. Explain yourself!'

'No time, I'm afraid,' Rollo said casually, shrugging his shoulders. 'Because soon there won't be a line to tread on. It'll have been eaten out of existence by the Deadly Dimension.'

'What izz thizzz Deadly Dimension?'

'Whoever is locked away in that closed sanctuary created it. It's nothing, really. I mean, it's a dimension of nothingness that eats away existence into nothing. And the more it eats, the more it expands, and the more it expands, the more it eats. It's moving pretty quickly. If it's not stopped, everything will be gone. All realities!'

'That is why communications are going down!' said the blackcurrant jelly creature. 'Those realities have been consumed. They're no longer there!'

'Correct!' shouted Rollo loudly. 'Now, if you excuse us, we're going to try and sort this out.'

'Security!' bellowed Pilate Vengling. The doors opened and four slarpups came pounding into the room.

Rollo put his arms around Dylan and Audrey.

'Cheerio!' he said to the room at large and just as the security guards reached them, they slipped with a pop and vanished from the room.

11

AFTER THE FAMILIAR darkness, they fell through the air. They weren't falling for long. Soon Dylan, Audrey and Rollo found themselves entangled in branches at different heights in a tree.

'Sorry!' called Rollo. 'I was in a rush. Miscalculated that last slip a bit.'

'You seem to be doing that quite a lot,' said Audrey, trying to manoeuvre herself into a safer position.

'Ha! I'd like to see you slip three people in a hurry. It's not like clicking your fingers.'

'Are we back?' asked Dylan, trying to get the leaves out of his face.

'Of course we're back in RTH-0709. Don't you know your own reality?'

'Not with my face full of leaves.'

Slowly they managed to clamber down from the tree. As Audrey pulled twigs from her hair, they looked around themselves. They were in Haling Grove.

'See. Back safe and sound.' Rollo adjusted his coat.

Dylan looked at the park. Everything was normal. A

plastic bag blew across the grass. A man and a woman were pushing their children on the swings in the play area. A woman was walking her dog on the perimeter of the park. They sky was overcast. He wondered if it was still the same day as the day they had left. The sky had been sunny when they gone into the well. How long had they been gone? It felt like ages, but there was no way of knowing.

'We're not safe though, are we?'

'How do you mean?' said Audrey, who had just finished pulling twigs from her hair.

'Well, if the Deadly Dimension is eating all realities out of existence, surely that includes ours too? How long before it gets to us?'

'I have a hunch that RTH-0709 is going to be the last reality to be swallowed,' said Rollo.

'A hunch? That's reassuring.' Audrey rolled her eyes.

'Where's that weird guy, the little one from the castle? Did he know anything?'
Rollo scratched his head.

'I don't know where he is now. After we slipped from the castle, he and I ended up here and you somewhere else. It didn't quite go right. I was a bit spent from slipping so many people at once in such stressful circumstances—it takes a lot out of you, you know—so I thought I'd grill him a bit more on what he knew about the Deadly Dimension. And then I went to try and find you guys. I didn't want to leave him in your reality unattended, so I took him with me to look for you but I lost him on the way. He could be in any reality. He might have been eaten by the Deadly Dimension already. I haven't the foggiest.'

'What did he say about the Deadly Dimension?'

'Not a lot. Except that he could feel its presence emanating from the entrance to your reality from his.'

'But if it was coming from here, *here* wouldn't exist, would it? The Deadly Dimension would have swallowed it?'

'Probably. It might not have been the Deadly Dimension itself he sensed from here— an echo maybe. Whatever it is—I think RTH-0709 is linked to it in some way. If we can find out how, it might give us a clue to what is going on.'

They were silent a moment.

'I think that we should be finding out what is up with Mr Ebenezer,' said Dylan. 'I'd gladly never see him again. But I think he meant for us to go through the well. Which means he must know about the existence of other realities at least. And he turned up when all of this started happening.'

'Good idea,' said Rollo, 'but first, I think some sustenance wouldn't be out of the question.'

They agreed to head to Croydon and find a café to get a bit to eat before heading back to the bookshop.

They decided on one of the cafés, upstairs in the one

of the high-street shopping centres, a small narrow one tucked into a corner. As they had left Haling Grove, Dylan asked Rollo what they were going to do about the fact that he didn't look human. Wouldn't people panic and call the police, or the local paper? Rollo said not to worry, no one would probably notice. He said that Dylan had probably noticed Rollo because everything had been stuckered when they met. Impossible to ignore the only other moving thing. Especially when it taps you on the shoulder. He said that in his experiences so far in RTH-0709, people had simply seemed uneasy when they looked in his direction and avoided looking into his eyes. Audrey pointed out that he didn't have any eyes.

Audrey and Rollo sat down at a table towards the back while Dylan got them coffee and sandwiches. As he placed the tray down at the table, he noticed a baby in a buggy nearby staring at Rollo and laughing. 'No manners,' said Rollo, who had noticed too. No one else in the café paid Rollo the slightest bit of attention. He had picked up his sandwich and was eyeing it with curiosity. 'This passes for food, does it?'

Neither Dylan or Audrey had yet picked up their food, too curious to see how Rollo would eat.

He was opening the sandwich and poking at its contents. 'What is it?'

'A sandwich,' said Audrey. 'It's two slices of bread with a filling in between. You've got brie and grapes.'

Rollo picked up a piece of grape from inside the sandwich and gave it an experimental squeeze between two of his long fingers. It popped out and landed in the coffee of the mother of the baby in the buggy. She was too deep in conversation to notice. The baby did though and gurgled with delight.

'Oops,' said Rollo. 'Let's give it a taste then.'

He took off his hat and stacked the two sandwich halves on top of his head. Dylan and Audrey looked at each other. Why was he fooling around? As they were about to tuck into their own sandwiches, there was a slight grating noise from Rollo. They looked back at him to see that a shallow crater had formed on top of his head. The sandwich was gradually lowered inside. A munching noise came from within.

'Hmm, not bad,' he said. The sandwich disappeared from sight and, with a popping noise, the indentation on his head popped back out so that it was a smooth unblemished dome again.

'What are you two staring at? Do you have no manners in this reality?'

Dylan and Audrey grew flustered and quickly started to eat their own food. Despite Rollo's protestations at being stared at, he himself seemed to be inspecting them as they ate, fixing his eyeless face on them in thoughtful silence. He waited for them to finish eating before he spoke.

'Once we've finished here, we'll head to Mr Ebenezer's shop. I've found nothing else on RTH-0709 that suggests any link to what's going on, apart from that shop's sudden appearance and your experiences.' He nodded at Dylan. 'We'll find out what he knows and then decide what's best to be done.' Dylan and Audrey nodded. Rollo put out one of his index fingers over the coffee in front of him.

'What's this?'

'Coffee,' said Dylan. 'It's a drink. It has caffeine in it.'

'I've not heard of caffeine. It smells good.' Rollo's finger trembled a little. He plunged it into the coffee.

'Careful! It's hot!' said Audrey.

Rollo didn't show any signs of being burnt. There was a slurping noise as his finger sucked up all of the coffee in one go. Pins and needles shot through Dylan.

'What's the matter?'

'Something weird is happening to Rollo.'

Rollo wasn't saying anything. His whole body started shaking.

'Maybe it was too much caffeine for someone who's not used to it.' There was an anxious tone in Audrey's voice.

Rollo continued to shake and barely moved otherwise. The lights in the café blacked out and came back on again instantly. In that split second a red and yellow snake appeared coiled around Rollo's neck, its tongue darting in and out, its eyes fixed on Dylan and Audrey. Its coils tightened. Audrey grabbed onto Dylan's arm. Slowly, as if Rollo's head was made of plasticine being moulded by unseen hands, creases and ridges formed in his face. A long nose appeared and then one eye and another, followed by a thin leering mouth as if an invisible knife was being drawn across the bottom of his face. It was wrinkled all over like an old apple.

Deep pupils appeared in the eyes. They rolled around left to right, as if searching. They finally settled on Dylan and Audrey and flicked between them as his expression became one big snarl.

'It's coming,' the face hissed. 'You'll be taken. Nothing! There'll be nothing left. The void... absorbed... The Deadly Dimension. He's breaking... The books...Helping us... Eeeer... Dylan...It cannot be helped.'

Dylan was sick with fright, but he forced himself to speak.

'Who are you? Who's helping you?'

There was no response. The face screwed itself up in pain.

'Corner! Stone. Giant?' it squealed. 'Even we are gone!'

And then Rollo's face was smooth and solid again. The snake uncoiled itself and slithered off indifferently. Rollo didn't move.

'Is he dead?' whispered Audrey.

'Well, he hasn't fallen apart this time.'

Dylan still felt the pins and needles. A llama wandered into the café, the other customers still not showing any sign of noticing the strange goings on.

'The llama from Mr Ebenezer's shop!' exclaimed Dylan.

It even had bits of book pages sticking out of its mouth. It ambled up to Rollo and stared at him, munching the paper as it did so. The pins and needles left Dylan. The llama too vanished.

Rollo shot up onto his feet.

'Oh! I like coffee!'

Dylan and Audrey stared at him.

'What's up with you two?'

'Erm, everything that just happened. Your face... you grew some *facial features*. And said some random things,' said Dylan.

'What kind of random things?'

They told him.

'Hmmm. I don't know what this means. But we must remember it. It's more of a lead than anything else we've encountered.'

'There was a llama too,' said Audrey, 'munching book pages.'

'A llama?'

'I saw it before. At Mr Ebenezer's shop.'

'The bookshop? And I mentioned books when I had that snake round my neck and was talking wildly... Come on. We've wasted enough time as it is.'

Rollo was already striding out of the coffee shop.

Croydon was as busy as ever as the weekend shoppers bustled about. Dylan was on edge as they walked. He expected something odd to happen, but nothing did. There were no pins and needles creeping up his body. It was just an ordinary afternoon on the high street. As they walked, Audrey was asking Rollo about what they ate and drank in his own reality. He used a lot of strange names of what he said were plants, and something that turned out to be a sort of cheese. And fish-like creatures. The closest thing to coffee they had, he said, was a drink made from liquid fossil fuels. But there was a furore as they were running out and hadn't yet worked out a method of making more that didn't take thousands of years. As he finished describing this drink, they turned onto the parade where Mr Ebenezer's shop was. They walked up to it and stopped outside. It looked even less open than usual. It wasn't just that the lights were off, the lack of anyone inside, or the *closed* sign. There was something foreboding. It seemed like it was a box that couldn't be opened.

Dylan walked up to the dusty glass and put his face up to it. He peered into the gloom. He could make out the stacks of books and the counter but there was no sign of Mr Ebenezer or anything unusual. Rollo came up beside him and peered in too.

'So where's the strange dark corner?'

'It's over there.' Dylan pointed to the back right corner of the shop. 'But it's further in, you can't see it from here.'

Rollo rapped his knuckles against the glass of the shop door four times. The sound of hard bone on glass was sharp. There was no sign of life in the shop. It was like Rollo was knocking on the glass of a museum cabinet.

After a few more moments of silence had passed, Rollo balled his hand into a fist and pounded on the wooden frame of the door. Not even the dust stirred on the other side.

'There's no one there,' said Audrey. 'Should we come back later? It's Mr Ebenezer we want to see.'

Dylan shook his head. 'Even if Mr Ebenezer isn't here, there's something weird about this shop. And everything weird seems to be connected to everything else. It might be better without Mr Ebenezer here, without him to watch what we're doing and stop us from finding out too much.'

Rollo was silent, arms folded.

'How do we get in? Smash the window with everyone around? Bust the lock?' Audrey was looking fed up.

That was a good point. Dylan reached out for the brass door knob and gave it a twist. It was locked of course, but you wouldn't know that unless you tried. He racked his brain.

'Rollo. Is there a way you could get in here? I mean, do you have a way of picking the lock… or can you transport us, I mean, *slip* us inside?'

'I could try slipping us inside. But it's risky. It's best to only slip inside buildings if you've been inside before, and are very sure of where you're going. Otherwise there's a strong possibility of slipping with half of yourself left behind in a wall or in some piece of furniture. Messy business. That isn't be so much of a problem for me, usually. Not to boast, but I'm a bit of an expert when it comes to slipping. I can do some things that few others are able to. But I've a funny feeling about this place. It feels like there's something in there which isn't too keen on me.' Rollo paused for a moment. 'It would be better if *you* slipped us in there, Dylan. I could give you a crash course. Usually, you would have to go on a year long course and pass your slipping test before it's safe, but we can't wait that long.'

Audrey looked scared.

'It will be dangerous,' said Dylan, 'but if we just sit around and wait, the Deadly Dimension might come and swallow us up. '

Audrey nodded.

'People vanishing out of thin air are harder to ignore than strange looking beings. Let's go over there by the bins and pigeons where we can do it without anyone noticing.'

Rollo explained that the way he was going to make them slip worked fine with jelli beings but that there seemed to be side affects for other creatures.

'Hopefully, you'll just feel a bit sick and maybe have a slight headache. Are you ready?'

Dylan didn't feel ready, but at the same time he was excited about trying to *slip* himself. That would be awesome.

Rollo put three long fingers on Dylan's head. They were surprisingly warm.

'You remember the dark place that we pass through every time we slip? That is called *outside*.'

Suddenly, Dylan felt that he was back in a strange but familiar darkness. He was inside his memory of the place—his eyes were open but he was seeing what Rollo was willing him to see. And it felt almost as horrible as being there.

'It is, as the name suggests, outside of all realties. If all the realities fit together like a globe—which they don't quite, but we won't go into that— *outside* would be like the space surrounding it. To slip, you need to go outside before you slip back down into where you want to be. Getting outside is the easy part of slipping. It's an instinctual thing, once you've got the feel for it. You just open up your mind and become oblivious to the reality your senses perceive. Basically to go *outside*, you tell your body to stop perceiving what's around you.'

Slowly a feeling was transmitted from Rollo's hand into Dylan's, a feeling that everything wasn't anything, at all. The people, the animals, the plants, the whole planet, the solar system, the universe and whatever lay beyond it was just a thought, a concept in his head, a passing imagination. A feeling of being disconnected came over him like a wave. Even his body was gone. There was just his consciousness, alone. Outside. Suddenly he was back again, standing amongst the bins and pigeons.

'That's the easy part,' said Rollo. 'You want to spend as little time as possible outside. Preferably not more than ten seconds. And certainly no more than five minutes. Any longer than that and your mind starts to forget about the existence of any reality and forgets that you ever even had a body. Once you get that far, you're more than likely to be stuck outside forever. Only a handful of people have been outside any longer than ten minutes and managed to come back. And when they have, let's just say that neither their minds or bodies were quite the same again. Understood?'

'Understood. So how do I get to where I want to be going from outside?'

'The way most people are trained to travel is through using known coordinates. It is the most reliable method and you don't have to have visited the destination before, but it's complicated and that's why it takes a year to study for your license. The other way of travelling is a lot simpler. If you've already been to the destination previously, you place your mind back in that reality using your memory. The better you remember the place, the easier it is to get there. As you concentrate on where you're going, you'll feel it becoming more tangible.

'You'll know if there's something not quite right. Whether you are about turn up inside a wall or if anything has changed since you were there or another being is standing directly where you're wanting to enter. If there's no blockage, just continue concentrating until you arrive in the reality, safe and sound. If there's a blockage, you must make adjustments to make sure you arrive in an open enough space. If there's no way in, you must return outside and change your destination immediately. The best thing to do is return to where you were coming from, to avoid being outside for longer than is safe.'

Rollo went through the basics of slipping a few more times with Dylan, using his hand to communicate the ideas and sensations so that Dylan had as much of an idea of it as possible.

'Time to give it a go then! Are you ready to *slip*, Master Thompson?'

Dylan nodded.

'But how do I take you and Audrey with me?'

'Just make sure you've got a firm grip on us as you slip. And imagine us being there when arriving at the other end.' Rollo turned to Audrey, who was looking highly sceptical. 'You needn't come if you're worried about being safe. You can wait outside the shop while we investigate.'

Audrey shook her head resolutely.

'I'm going wherever Dylan's going. I'm not being left behind. I just wish there was a safer way of doing things.'

'Fine. Ready, Dylan?'

Dylan held Audrey's hand tightly and gave it a reassuring squeeze. He grabbed Rollo's hand in his other.

'Ready.'

He closed his eyes and started to distance himself from the reality around him in the way that Rollo had told him. It wasn't at all easy. There were the sounds of cars passing, planes in the sky and pigeons cooing, together with the smell of the bins and gravity pushing him to the ground. Reality had him in its grip. How could he block all of that out?

'Stop tensing. Take it easy. It will not be fast, the first time. Let your mind leave your senses behind momentarily, but don't force it. Let it happen gradually.'

Dylan stopped pushing himself so much. He thought about the places he'd been since he had moved back to Croydon. Realities other than the one he was standing in. Realities that felt like they were they only ones, each to itself. He remembered being in the house that he and Rollo had found themselves in when they followed Audrey into the well in Haling Grove. He recalled the dim light and the room full of a jumble and the owl flying out of the plate. A real memory, but not from this existence. As he explored this feeling, the less solid the reality in front of him felt. And, slowly, he started drifting away from what was immediately around him. He let go of the streets of Croydon, the sights, sounds and smells. He let go of the Earth and gravity, the moon and the stars and everything beyond them. Finally, the idea of his body was gone and suddenly he realised he was outside, in that dark space where he had been when they slipped before. He turned his mind to their destination. He imagined himself, Audrey and Rollo appearing in Mr Ebenezer's bookshop, focusing on the spot directly in front of the counter, where there would be enough space for all of them to re-enter reality. He pictured the counter, the chair behind it, the record player and the books piled up on either side of where they would appear, the greyness of the ceiling and the smell of dusty pages that would greet them. It didn't take long for the scene in his imagination to start to feel more solid, the sensation of having a body beginning to return. He didn't feel there was any barrier to them arriving, no other bodies or furniture that might be in their way. He made sure he imagined the others with him in the bookshop. And then they were there. He opened his eyes and he was standing in the bookshop clutching Audrey and Rollo's hands. He felt dizzy and exhilarated. He had *slipped*! And not just himself, but two other people.

'Good work, Dylan!' Rollo patted him on the back. 'Most impressive for your first time. Maybe you'll get to work on it again if we manage not to get eaten by the Deadly Dimension. Speaking of which, let's have a good look around.'

'What are we looking for?' asked Audrey bewildered.

'Anything. Look for anything unusual, or that sticks out.'

'Everything's unusual in here,' said Dylan, looking around. Audrey found the light switch. The air felt like it hadn't been disturbed in months, although it had only been the day before that they had been asking Mr Ebenezer about odd goings on around Croydon.

Nothing struck them as they looked round. There was the till, the huge catalogue of the books, the record player and a stack of records on the floor beneath the shelf it stood on. The drawers in the counter were empty. There was nothing else. No handwritten notes, nothing even in the wastepaper basket. All that was left to contemplate was the books.

'The dark corner is over there, is it?' Rollo pointed in the direction Dylan had indicated earlier. He started walking towards the passageway of books, managing a few strides before letting out a moan and collapsing.

He he had gone limp.

'Help me back towards the entrance. I've gone floppy.'

As soon as they dragged him away from the sinister passage, he quickly revived.

'What's up with those books?' whispered Rollo. Cautiously, he began to walk back. As soon as he got to close to the books, he drew back.

'It's like some kind of barrier pushing me away.'

'Mr Ebenezer was very particular about the order of the books,' explained Dylan. 'He got me to re-arrange a load of them in a specific pattern. It seemed bizarre. Maybe the way the books are arranged is creating some kind of protective field.'

'I wonder what's he protecting,' whispered Audrey to herself.

'I'm glad you two are using those brains of yours. If only I could get down to that corner to try and work out what's going on.'

'Well, Dylan, you were down there before, weren't you?' said Audrey. 'Maybe it only keeps out people from other realities. Or maybe it wasn't keeping *you* out. Or maybe it was that Mr Ebenezer took you down there.'

'There's only one way to find out. Perhaps it will work if we all three go there.'

They walked to the passageway and down it a short way.

'Doesn't seem to have any effect on us.'

'I'll wait here,' said Rollo. 'Have a look at that corner and see what you make of it.'

'Is there anything we should be looking out for?' asked Audrey.

'If the llama appears, or any other creature for that matter, try talking to it. See if it has anything to say. Be careful. If you suddenly get a weird feeling of danger coming from somewhere, throw something where that feeling is coming from. But not one of the books. I don't think it's a good idea to mess with Mr Ebenezer's barrier. We don't know what harm it might do. For all we know, it might be keeping something *in* rather than *out*. Something that might cause a lot of trouble, if it got out. Here is something for you to throw.'

Rollo took out what looked like a dark stone from his pocket and handed it to Dylan.

'What is it?' He held it up to the light.

'It's a kind of tracking device. Standard Intrapelatio issue. Pretty expensive. They probably wouldn't like it being thrown into unknown dark voids, but what, ho... They're already annoyed with me anyway, can't make it much worse.'

Dylan popped the tracking device into his pocket.

'See you in a minute, hopefully.'

Dylan and Audrey made their way into the passage, Dylan leading the way. He could remember the way from the time he had come to assist Mr Ebenezer. Again, it felt like there shouldn't be so many passages in a bookshop of its size. As they got closer to the corner of the shop, a creeping feeling came over them, as if they were being watched. There was no one on either side, but the nearer they got to the corner, the more the feeling increased. Before long, they were holding hands. They both stopped dead when they turned the corner that led to the dark spot. It felt like it was pushing back at them like a magnet pushing away another magnet of the same polarity.

They gripped each other's hands tighter and walked towards the darkness until they got to the books directly in front of it.

Dylan pulling out the tracking device that Rollo had given him.

'Be ready to run if something bad happens.'

'Don't worry, I'm set to go. This place is giving me the creeps.'

'Right. Here goes.'

Dylan flung the stone like object up into the darkness. There was no sound of it hitting the wall, or dropping down onto the floor. If the darkness led to somewhere else, the device had gone through it.

'Let's get out of here,' said Audrey moving away.

Just as Dylan was about to follow, something caught his eye. The title of one of the books in the stacks in front of the dark corner, *Unusual Land Animals of No Small Consequence*. Not thinking, he reached out and touched the spine. Different realities existing was one thing, but books whose title you had made up? He couldn't just leave it there. Mr Ebenezer had said that it was his, if he found it. And he had. He would regret it if he left it. It felt important that he took it. Slowly, he slid the book out so as not to disturb the other volumes around it.

'Dylan! What are you doing?'

Dylan looked round to see Audrey's look of bafflement, which turned to one of horror as she looked back towards the dark corner. Looming out of the shadow was the snake he'd first seen what seemed like an age ago.

'Hey,' said Dylan.

'What are you doing?' hissed Audrey. 'Talking to snakes!'

'Rollo said to talk to any creature you meet, didn't he?'

'It doesn't look like it wants to talk!'

Dylan tried again. 'S-sorry if we disturbed you. What's the dark space behind you?'

The snake swayed and blinked its eyes, tongue flicking but it didn't so much as hiss. Dylan went closer but stayed out of reach of its swaying head.

'Dylan!'

'What were you doing in my bathroom sink? All this started when I saw you through the plughole. And now you're here.'

Dylan took a step back. The snake bared its fangs, darting towards him. Dylan tried to hit it with the book he was holding. The snake's fangs narrowly avoided his wrist, closing around the book. Dylan waved the book around in the air but the snake held on with its powerful jaws, its colourful tail swirling round his head.

'Just drop the book!' screamed Audrey, ducking out of the way. Rollo was trying to shout something to them from back at the shop entrance, but Dylan couldn't make it out. He wasn't going to lose the book. It felt important. The snake released its jaws to have another chance at biting him.

They ran as fast as they could around the passages, but the snake kept close behind, slithering along at an alarming speed.

'Pull the books down in its way,' shouted Audrey.

He knew he shouldn't do it. Rollo had told him not to. But what other chance did they have against a vicious looking snake from another reality?

They started pulling books down as they went. It slowed the snake down, but it was still pursuing them, slithering its black, red and yellow coils across the books.

They followed the route they had come, but it was longer than it should have been. Dylan remembered there was no trusting the insides of this shop to be straightforward. Although they weren't finding the way back to the entrance, he could see it there just beyond the row of books. But somehow they couldn't get there. Every passage seemed to lead somewhere else. They would have to force themselves through. Dylan grabbed hold of Audrey and together they rolled into the piles of books, crashing them down everywhere, tumbling over them onto the floor. They found themselves in front of the main door.

They were back on their feet in an instant. There was no sign of Rollo. The snake had risen up behind the books and wasn't going to waste time pursuing them. They rushed out. Dylan slammed the door behind them.

'Wasn't it locked?' asked Audrey.

Everywhere looked different. Across the road was a sign for Aldgate East tube station. The pavement was full of people, heavy traffic filled the street. Puzzled, they looked at each other.

'We're not even in Croydon!' said Audrey.

Dylan looked at the door behind him. An unfamiliar door to a dark and empty shop with a mound of post piled up at the bottom. That wasn't Mr Ebenezer's shop. He tried the door handle. It was locked.

'Rollo! Where is Rollo?', shouted Dylan.

'*Slip* us back to Croydon! We need to see what's going on.'

Dylan shook his head.

'What if I mess it up? I can't do it without Rollo. And what if we end up straight back in front of that snake again?'

They agreed it would be safest to go back to Croydon on public transport rather than to try *slipping* on their own just yet. Strangely, they didn't really feel shaken surprised at having been moved across London suddenly.

As they entered the tube station, Dylan realised he was still clutching the book. There were a few other people waiting on the platform, but it wasn't too busy, considering the bustle of the street above. The next tube was in six minutes' time, so they wandered down the platform and found a bench. Dylan looked at the paperback in his hands, *Unusual Land Animals of No Small Consequence*. He would have expected some interesting illustrations on the front with a title like that, but it was a plain off-white background with a geometric pattern in the middle. He didn't open it to look inside. There was already enough running around his brain—he would save this for later. After a few minutes had passed, the tell-tale rumblings of the approaching tube train came from the tunnel. A low *oooooom* layered with *chm-ka-chm-ka-chm-ka-chm-ka*.

Pins and needles spread through Dylan's body.

'Oh no!' he shouted out loud, looking around to see what was out of place.

'What?'

Dylan didn't answer.

There was the noise of the tube and the the screeching of what sounded like metal grinding against metal. It was unnervingly familiar.

As the tube train rushed into the station, he saw a tear opening in a mass of darkness that seemed to be floating further down the platform. Audrey saw it too.

'The Deadly Dimension!' shouted Audrey.

'No, it can't be!'

A man with a rhinoceros horn emerged from the dark mass. Slarpups. Three more slipped out after the first. They looked around the station urgently, as if searching. Just as the doors to the tube slid open, one of them pointed at Dylan and Audrey and bellowed.

All eyes were on their monstrous faces and strong limbs as they charged down the platform heading for the train amidst screams. Quickly Audrey and Dylan jumped into the carriage.

'Close, damn it, close,' whispered Audrey to the doors. The slarpups looked ferocious. They were coming nearer and nearer. It felt like forever. Dylan and Audrey's hearts pounded. There wasn't anywhere for them to hide or go.

Suddenly, with the slarpups just metres away, with a sudden hiss of air, the doors slid closed. Just as the tube was moving away, one of them pounded on the door. Some of the passengers screamed while others looked on in shock at the tusked creature assaulting the train. Its fists were powerful and soon a crack appeared in the glass but the tube was picking up speed and the slarpups were left, chasing the accelerating train down the platform, until it disappeared into the darkness of the tunnel.

The people in the train chattered in confusion. What had they just seen? Some were trembling and holding their hands up to their mouths. Dylan could hear some people saying that it must be a publicity stunt, people dressed up with rhino masks.

Both Audrey and Dylan were white as sheets. The people around them had begun to quieten down. Must be a publicity stunt, or a party. By the time the tube had reached the next stop and other people got on without anything unusual happening, the chatter died down and people continued their journeys as if nothing had happened. The encounter was so brief that they they began question whether it had really happed at all. In their memories, the faces of the creatures looked a lot less realistic, much more like rubber masks. Very convincing though. It was impressive, what could be done these days. They avoided looking at the cracked pane of glass in the door. The new passengers eyed it with suspicion, but they wouldn't have imagined that it had been caused by the pounding of a horned man from another reality.

Dylan and Audrey sat there frozen in horror. At every one of the remaining eight stops, they expected to see the slarpups reappear. But each time the doors opened and shut and nothing out of the ordinary happened as the train departed. Fifteen minutes later they arrived at Victoria.

The station was heaving with people. Dylan and Audrey made their way to the boards showing the train times to see when the next one was to East Croydon. Dylan saw something out of the corner of his eye. There appeared to be a gorilla serving burgers in the food stall to their right. He looked around for anything else out of the ordinary. A man with the head of a fly and greasy looking wings poking out of the back of his jacket was begging people for change for a cup of tea, rubbing his feelers together nervously.

Something even weirder was just about to happen. He knew it.

'There's a train in four minutes, platform 15,' said Audrey. 'Let's get it.'

Dylan shook his head.

'Something's going to happen.'

'Like what? If it's the slarpups, shouldn't we get out of here?'

'Even if it's them, I want to see what they're after.'

'What if they want us dead or captured?'

'I'll slip us out of trouble. They won't expect that.'

'I'm not sure you *will* be able to do that. You said you wouldn't earlier. You've only done it once before, and that was when Rollo was with us.'

'You don't have to stay,' said Dylan. 'I want to find out about the Deadly Dimension. It's scary and exciting. Anyway, we won't be safe anywhere—nowhere in the world when that wave of darkness devours our reality.'

'I'm not going to leave you to get butchered by weird creatures! What kind of friend would I be, if I did that? Fine. We'll see what's going on. And try to stay in one piece.' She was pale and trembling but she still had that firm look in her eye, determination lurking in her expression. He took her hand.

'Let's go up there.' Dylan pointed at the balcony above some shops where there were bars and restaurants.

They went up to the balcony. They watched the crowd down below them. People were moving around each other in their own bubbles of reality. As well as entirely separate realities existing, each person had their own personal reality. Only they were experiencing what was in front of them, through their own eyes. People's experiences were never exactly the same and never would be.

Pins and needles shot through his body much more strongly than he had experienced before. He felt rooted to the spot. Every single person below them and around them froze completely. Every pigeon flapping through the station hung in mid-air, as if the pause button on the remote for the world had been pressed. *Stuckered*, as Rollo had said in Convent Garden on Dylan's birthday. Dylan tried to move, but the pins and needles still paralysed him. He hoped that he wasn't stuckered too, or Audrey. He couldn't even move his mouth to ask her if she was OK.

With everything stuckered, the constant murmur of people, machinery, shop music and trains was completely silenced. Suddenly, into that silence came that awesome sound of grinding metal. He knew what to expect: a dark mass like a ball made of a strange substance that would disgorge menacing creatures through a slit or a tear that appeared suddenly.

There it was below them, a strange darkness hovering just above the crowd below. The darkness seemed to be opening up, there was a slit in its belly slowly growing till it had become big enough to disgorge the four slarpups that had appeared at Aldgate East. They scanned the area and didn't take long to discover Dylan and Audrey standing at the centre of the balcony in front of them. They split up into twos in the direction of the stairs that led up to either end of the balcony.

Dylan tried frantically to move, but he was still stuck-ered. This hadn't happened the first time. Now they were in danger. It was all his fault. His fault Audrey had stayed in the station instead of going home. And what could they do now? What was going to happen to them? And how would his dad feel if his son vanished into thin air? He felt sick.

As the slarpups got to the foot of the stairs, there was a pop behind Dylan.

'What are you two standing around for!'

It was Rollo! He laid a hand on both Dylan and Audrey's shoulders. After a moment, sensation returned to their bodies and they could move.

The slarpups had paused at the bottom of the stairs. They recognised Rollo and seemed wary. Almost scared of him. What sort of person or creature was Rollo to inspire such feelings in those horrible creatures? After a moment they started to very slowly ascend the stairs.

'Can you slip us somewhere out of their reach, Rollo?'

'They've locked this place down somehow to try and stop anyone slipping in or out. I had a hard time getting in. I don't think they've any reason to do us harm. I *think* anyway. They might try and take us away. But they know who I am.'

'Who are you? Why are they scared?'

'I'm your friend. Among other things.'

'It's the *other* things that I mean.'

The slarpups got to the top of the stairs and began heading towards them from either side, stopping a few metres away as if waiting for orders.

'Alright, chaps?' asked Rollo.

'Rollovkarghjicznilegogh-Vylpophyngh, I am DI Bartleby of the slarpups IntraPolice. We have been sent to arrest this boy of unknown species on suspicion of creating the Deadly Dimension. We are also to arrest you and the girl for acting as accessories to the act.'

'What?' shouted Audrey, forgetting her fear, as the slarpups didn't appear to be wanting to do any violence to them. 'Dylan's just a boy. We didn't even know there were other realities until a few days ago. How on Earth would we know how to create a Deadly Dimension?'

'We have been gathering information. We've detected

that a way into the closed sanctuary exists in RTH-0709, and its connected to this boy in some way. We believe a sanctuary is the only place something as powerful as the Deadly Dimension could be created.'

'I barely know anything about sanctuaries,' said Dylan. 'I only know what Rollo told me. And as Audrey said, we didn't know any other realities existed until now. How and why would I create something to destroy things that I didn't even know existed?'

'You are the only suspect and will be arrested and taken in for questioning.' said DI Bartleby, clearly not in the mood for discussing things.

All four of the IntraPolice moved towards the trio, but stopped short to listen when there was a weird squeaking sound in the air, like a balloon being tortured.

'Someone else is trying to get in.' said Rollo. 'And doing a pretty messy job of it.'

The air around them felt strange and the squeaking noise climaxed into a quick succession of pop, pop.

Next to them appeared Pilate Gerskin, the blackcurrant jelly person, and a woman with the head of a vulture from the Intrapelatio Union.

'Bzzzzzzbartleby! What is the meaning of this?' shouted a furious Pilate Gerskin. 'This reality has been stuckered and locked without authorisation. The slar-pups must stop taking things into their own hands. Again, *bzzzzz*, what it is the meaning of this?!'

DI Bartleby was not phased. 'This boy is suspected of creating the Deadly Dimension and possibly closing the sanctuary.'

All three of the IU councillors looked at Dylan curiously.

'Bzzzzreally? He doesn't look capable.'

'He isn't!' shouted Audrey.

'Either way, Bartleby, this is a disgrace. The IU knows nothing of this. You cannot behave in this way. Stuckering realities and trying to arrest its inhabitants with no authorisation whatsoever.' Pilate Gerskin rubbed his feelers together as he thought over the situation. 'Rollo, you must cease being so secretive and start providing the information we employ you to deliver. You will come back to the IU hub with us.'

Rollo was strangely silent.

'Bartleby, you will unstucker this place and join us. We will discuss the plans we have drawn together, and alter them according to whatever information you have been holding back, Rollo.'

'What about the boy?' demanded Bartleby.

The jelly-like person piped up in a voice much more solid than he looked. 'The boy should not be taken yet. There are many intricate regulations regarding taking custody of citizens of a newly tapped reality. These two children were taken into custody before, but only when they were intruding outside of RTH-0709. We will come back for him when authorisation has been agreed.'

'I understand that. But if this boy is the creator of the Deadly Dimension, he may be able to stop it. Either way, he should be held accountable. Are you really suggesting we simply let the child go, so he can wreak even more havoc?'

'Are you suggesting we simply ignore the normal protocol, Bartleby? I shouldn't be too surprised—you don't seem to have too much respect for the IU regulations.'

'Respect, Ignatius? This is not a question of respect! It's about the safety of all realities. The normal rules cannot apply. Pilate Gerskin, can you not see this?'

Pilate Gerskin buzzed angrily. 'Bzzzzzzzz…whether you are right or wrong, it is not for you decide,' he shouted. 'The more time we waste here, the more likely we are to get swallowed by the Deadly Dimension!'

He carried on speaking, but Dylan didn't catch the rest of what he said as Audrey was pulling on his shirt sleeve. He looked over at her. She put a finger to her lip to make sure he kept quiet and pointed discreetly at the train times on the board. There was a train back to East Croydon in twenty seconds' time. Dylan looked away, but Audrey tugged on his sleeve again. Dylan looked back. He wasn't sure what he was supposed to be looking at, but he kept looking. After a while, time changed from 17:03:07 to 17:03:08. Time was moving! He looked around the station. If he concentrated on a couple of people, he could see that rather than being as still as they seemed, they were actually moving, very, very slowly. Audrey leaned over and whispered in his ear, 'Shall we run?'

Dylan looked at the others. They were still arguing and a lot of arm waving was going on. He was sure that Rollo was trying to gesture discreetly for them to go.

He grabbed Audrey's hand and started running. They hadn't got far, before they heard shouts behind them. They didn't look back, but concentrated on avoiding bumping into people who, only just unstuckered, were heading slowly towards the platforms. Pins and needles fizzed through Dylan without warning. What might happen? Could they really have more strange events in store? The hand and wrist of a man they passed sprouted into flowers and there were stalks bursting out of his shirt sleeves. In a glance, they saw that his head was beginning to sprout a giant head of corn.

Similar things were happening to other people. A woman who had been shouting and arguing suddenly had a gush of water coming out of her mouth and turned into a fountain. A stall that had been selling baguettes was now offering giant stick insects. A man who looked pretty normal, apart from his elephant-like trunk, was happily stuffing a number of them into a large carrier bag.

The train was in front of them, just about to leave, but

the doors were still open. They ran, jumping onto it, just as they were sliding shut. The slarpups were clambering over the barriers. The train wasn't yet moving. Even if it did, there would be time for them to catch up, if time didn't get back to normal speed. Everything was still a bit stuckered.

'Come on, come on. Go!' shouted Audrey.

A grinding noise filled the air. Above the platform a cloud of something dark had appeared. They could hear it being ripped apart. Just as the slarpups made it over the barriers followed by the Intrapelatio Union members, the cloud disgorged a huge lump of something grey onto the platform. It looked like a bag made of elephant skin. Hundreds of long tentacles started growing out of it, reaching for the slarpups who, brandishing whips, cautiously stepped back, looking defensive. The Intrapelatio Union members faced the creature for what seemed an age, Pilate Gerskin's bee-like fuzz was covered in beads of sweat. Fear rippled across their faces and they vanished into thin air. Dylan couldn't see Rollo anywhere.

One of the tentacles of the monster had succeeded in getting a grip on a slarpup, but the other slarpups managed to get their whips wound round the bulk of the beast. As they tightened their grip, the ropes glowed blue and crackled. The creature let out a piercing cry and dropped the officer it was holding. He soon recovered and added his efforts to controlling it. They shouted something to each other. The tear in the dark cloud above the platform closed but at the same time another opened in the pavement below, sucking all into it and closing with a pop.

The doors finally closed in a rush. All around them, people were moving at normal speed. An automated voice announced the destination and stops. The train began to move.

'It's not something you get used to, is it?' said Audrey. 'One minute, all this weird stuff is happening, but it feels real, almost normal…and then, just as suddenly, everything goes back to how it usually is. That's when you feel peculiar, and all the stuff that just happened begins to feel like a dream.'

Dylan shot her a look.

'Oh, I'm not saying it was a dream. It's too late for that. And if it isn't real, then I'm going mad, we're both going mad.'

They looked at the other passengers and out of the train windows. Nothing out of the ordinary. Not until the person sitting opposite them lowered his paper, revealing a shiny ostrich egg head.

'Rollo!'

'Yes, that's me.'

'Rollo,' said Dylan, 'can I ask you a question? It's about you, and it's been on my mind for a while.'

'No time!' Rollo said tersely. 'The IU councillors back there, did you see them vanish?'

'Yes… when the big grey thing appeared, they got out of there pretty quickly,' said Audrey.

'Ah, it may have looked like they were running from the garble bag, but they weren't. They wouldn't, not when the slarpups were there to deal with it. Gerskin received an emergency intra-real transmission. I didn't catch all of it, but it was from the control room at the Intra-Travel Guild. There's something homing in on your reality's coordinates. That it was stuckered for so long made RTH-0709 suddenly very visible to anyone or thing looking for it. They didn't seem to know what is coming this way, but I caught the words 'huge', 'terrifying' and 'wouldn't hang around'.'

'The Deadly Dimension!' Dylan's eyes widened. If it was on its way to their reality, what chance did they have to stop it?

'Well… Maybe. It could be the Deadly Dimension. We know very little about it. But one thing that has been consistent is that it has been expanding steadily in all directions, not showing any sign of consciousness or being controlled by another being. It would be unusual for it to suddenly home in on one place in particular. Unless there was something in that place that was attracting it like a magnetic force. But it could be something else entirely. Either way, the words 'huge' and 'terrifying' don't bode well, I fear.'

'If the Intrapelatio people left in such a hurry, whatever

is coming is probably going to come soon, right? What can we do?' Audrey's face was white with fear.

'Not very much,' replied Rollo, still not sounding particularly worried, 'except for keeping our eyes and ears open. And our senses. Feeling any tingles, Dylan?'

Dylan shook his head. He didn't feel anything. Other than Rollo's presence, it seemed like a normal train journey. People were reading free papers, tinny music bled from headphones and electronic devices were being fiddled with. Reality seemed solid enough outside the the train too.

The train stopped at Clapham Junction and a number of people got on and off. The next station would be East Croydon.

'We'll need to go back to Mr Ebenezer's shop when we get back,' said Dylan. 'It all started there. We haven't a clue what's going on, apart from that place.'

12

A COUPLE OF MINUTES before they were due to arrive at East Croydon station, there was the sound of a loud thunder clap that peeled for an extraordinary length of time. Dylan covered his ears. Everything in his vision was stretched, distorted and confused like in a dream. On Audrey's neck sat Rollo's smooth oval head, while her head lay disembodied in in Rollo's lap. As soon as Dylan cried out, their heads were back in their proper places.

Everywhere there was confusion but curiously many didn't seem shocked by what was happening and were trying quite calmly to carry on. Some people were stuckered, while others had become intermingled with objects around them. One man's torso had become the newspaper that he had been holding and he was trying to bend his head to carry on reading it. The woman next to him had become a mish mash of her normal body parts, mixed with that of a fly. Hands, feelers, bug eyes and human eyes were all mixed up. A teenage boy who had been standing up, holding on to the rail, now had an arm that was part of the rail. Outside the window, patches of darkness kept appearing and disappearing, some revealing views of what must be other realities – strange spires of glistening cities, red mountains under purple skies, the beach where Dylan and Audrey had been captured by the crab people. For a brief moment, they were speeding along next to another train made of something completely transparent, and all of its passengers were like Rollo.

'Jelli beings!' shouted Dylan.

Rollo spun round to look and put his hand to the window. A small jelli being—a child it looked like—was waving at them from the train in Rollo's reality. Then the window between realities was gone and replaced by other images. Outside, things in their own reality were being warped and changed. Office buildings were stretched and bent in weird directions, splintered and fanned out like fir cones. On some, huge faces appeared, looking around in confusion. Up in the sky were humungous cucumbers, flying along with wings made of fish like bizarre planes.

'Are we too late?' asked Dylan. 'Is all lost?'

His question met with an awesome silence. Both Audrey and Rollo were lost for words. This was something entirely new. It wasn't just people from other realities appearing in their own, or being stuckered, this was normal reality being mutated and twisted on a mass scale, as if all of the rules had been broken.

As they approached East Croydon station, the rails suddenly twisted and the train turned upside down as they entered the station. Each of them managed to grab onto something and land the right way up as the ceiling became the floor of the carriage.

'East Croydon this is... is this East Croydon? I think this is East Croydon. If you wish to chance it, please change here,' said the electronic voice over the tannoy.

'That's reassuring,' said Audrey.

The doors opened. They were hanging down from the ceiling of the train and had to let themselves drop down and onto the platform. The people boarding the train were jumping up and trying to pull themselves up onto it, as if that were entirely normal.

Audrey, Dylan and Rollo hastened up the platform and up the slopes leading to the entrance of the station. When they got the top, the place was deserted. They exited the station and discovered that there were no people around at all. A few buses, a tram and some cars were standing still in the road, with no sign of any passengers. Apart from that, everything on the ground was as normal, but in the air they caught glimpses of other realities and strange patches of darkness.

'Come on. Let's get back to Ebenezer's bookshop, if we can,' said Dylan.

'Keep your wits about yourselves,' said Rollo. 'It's not too far from here is it? Let's take it slow and hope that we remain the right shape and in the right reality. I've never heard of occurrences such as these, not anywhere. I would slip us, but I don't want to risk it with all this going on. Something is seriously up. And down. And every other direction and back again.'

The three of them slowly started walking along the pavement, looking carefully around. They walked a hundred metres or so before anything strange happened, other than the flickering views of other realities. A sound caused them all to stop dead in their tracks. It was a scrunching, rubbly dusty sound. They looked behind them to see a rough cement statue in the shape of a man that appeared to have sprouted from the ground.

'Hello!' said Rollo cheerfully. 'Can we help you, Mr Cement Man?' The cement man didn't move. 'Doesn't look like he's going to bother us.'

'Just a bit creepy,' said Audrey as they turned to carry on.

As they did so, there were a lot more scrunching, rubbly sounds. They looked back to see at least another thirty or forty cement figures rising out of the pavement. The one Rollo had dubbed Mr Cement Man raised a finger to point at them. A lot of dust fell from his joints as he did so.

'I think maybe we should forget my suggestion of being slow. Walk fast!'

'Shouldn't we go faster... I mean run?' said Audrey.

'I don't think they're going to be that fast. We might as well carry on being cautious. Let's just keep an eye on them.'

Rollo was right. The cement people came stumbling after them at a slow walking pace.

They walked down the street that East Croydon station is on and that leads to the centre of town. As they passed a gap in the buildings on the other side of the road, they saw that there were even more cement people stumbling towards them.

'I don't like this,' said Audrey.

'Just keep going and keep your wits about you,' replied Rollo looking round cautiously.

At the end of the street, they saw more cement people coming. Some raised their cement fingers to point at them. They began to run towards the bookshop which wasn't far away in St George's Walk. The cement people picked up their pace too, but were still a lot slower. A couple overexerted themselves and fell to the ground, smashing bits of their limbs off in clouds of dust, struggling to get back up.

They got to the end of St George's Walk and stopped. It was full of cement people turning to face them.

'We can't go down there! There's too many,' said Audrey, catching her breath.

Dylan thought quickly.

'Queens Gardens!' he said. 'It's a long shot, but maybe

they don't like grass and mud. It's been raining so much that it's all slippery and wet. They'll fall and break.'

'Not much choice!' shouted Rollo as the cement people in St. George's Walk started moving towards them, and those that were already chasing them were closing the gap.

They ran again, Dylan leading them to the gardens, which were not far away at all. In front of their path, more and more cement people kept appearing.

'Dodge them,' shouted Rollo.

'But…' started Audrey.

There were surrounded. They had no choice but to run. Dylan ran in front. He ducked and weaved past the figures in front of them, just avoiding the last one's attempt to grab him by skidding underneath his arms down on to the gravel path of the park. He heard a loud cry behind him and leapt to his feet.

Both Audrey and Rollo had been caught. They were struggling to free themselves from the cement hands that gripped them, but they were too tight.

Dylan sprinted back towards them, but as he reached them, Rollo managed to push him with his free arm so he rolled back down the path.

'You can't save us, Dylan!' He shouted. 'Too late! You have to save yourself, you have to…' As he said the last word, a cracking sound filled the air. Both he and Audrey turned a horrible grey, clothes and all, and hardened until they were like the grey cement figures surrounding them.

Dylan cried out in anguish. His friends! Tears welled up behind his eyes, but didn't fall. He had to save himself. The cement people, including what had been Audrey and Rollo started making their way towards him. He had to save himself. Maybe he could put things back the right way. He didn't know how, but there was no chance for the world, if they got hold of him too. What had Rollo been trying to say? He sprung to his feet and ran down the path and onto the grass till he reached the middle of the lawn.

The cement people slowly came down the path towards him. They edged up to the grass and stopped. He was right! They didn't like the grass. It filled them with fear. It had been a long shot but he was right. He looked around. There were cement people coming from every direction. He couldn't think what to do next. As he frantically tried to think, the cement people lined up along every edge of the lawn.

What he had to do hit him. He must slip. Maybe that's what Rollo had been trying to say. He hadn't wanted to himself, but even if it was dangerous to do so, what other choice was there? He looked up. Patches of the sky were alternatively showing views of total darkness and other realities. Who knew where he would end up, if he did slip.

He looked at the cement people. The ones nearest to the grass were tentatively placing their feet onto it. At first, they recoiled at the springy, unsolid feel of it. But they didn't give up. Eventually one placed its whole foot tentatively on the grass and leaned its whole weight on it. Soon, some of others did the same.

Very slowly they advanced onto the grass. Nervously at first, but then they grew in confidence and started to move ever so slightly faster, and with more intent. 'I've got no choice. I've got to,' Dylan said to himself.

He closed his eyes and tried to calm himself. He breathed deeply, cleared his mind and focused on the inside of Mr Ebenezer's shop. After a few moments, he felt pins and needles start to tingle over his body and the feeling that he was being pulled towards something. Just at the last moment, the image of Audrey and Rollo turning into cement filled his consciousness. And he lost it. He opened his eyes. The cement people were about ten metres away.

'This is it,' he thought. 'But you can do it!'

He closed his eyes and tried again. After a few seconds, he felt the same pins and needles and tugging feeling. He swore he could smell the old books from the shop when another image of someone entered his mind.

'Dad!' he shouted.

If this was all going on, what was happening to his dad? He opened in his eyes. The cement people were right in front of him and making to grab him. He breathed in sharply, closed his eyes, focusing his mind on where he wanted to go. And, in an instant, he was gone. The hands of the cement people closed upon thin air.

Dylan opened his eyes. He had done it! He had slipped. But he wasn't in Mr Ebenezer's shop. He was standing in the hallway of his house, right by the front door. 'Dad!' He shouted. 'Where are you? Dad!'

He ran up the stairs, calling out. He checked every room upstairs, came back down and ran back to the kitchen. He wasn't there, or in the garden. He ran back to check the front room, the only remaining place he could be.

He opened the door. Rather than finding the familiar room with a sofa, arm chairs, the coffee table and TV, he found the inside of Mr Ebenezer's shop. The jazz music that had been playing the first time he went in was drifting over from the corner. The books were piled up in their mysterious stacks. All the ones he and Audrey had pulled down were back in their usual places. He looked behind him. The hallway was still there. He couldn't see Mr Ebenezer.

He looked out of the window. It was the street his house was on, not St George's walk. To his dismay, it was full of cement people, all making their way to the house. He heard loud thudding on the front door. He put his head to the window pane and craned to see what was going on. A group of cement people were pummelling the door, trying to break it down. He heard a crack as it started to splinter. The cement people noticed his face at the glass and pointed at him. They forgot the door and started for the window. They would shatter it in seconds! He stood back. If they got in, he would run down the path between the piles of books. Maybe even run into the dark corner where he had thrown Rollo's tracking device.

Some cement people raised their fists to smash the glass. Dylan's body tingled with pins and needles, and he momentarily felt like he was about to pass out. The cement people still had their fists in the air, but they hadn't brought them down. They were all looking at something behind them. They began to head in different directions, as if they couldn't make up their minds which way they should be going. Through the window, he could see a solid darkness in the sky, terrifying and completely unlike the patches of darkness he had seen previously. It was a different darkness, more like what had appeared at the castle where Audrey had been trapped, more like... Yes, that's what it was... definitely... the Deadly Dimension!

It was here! There was nothing he could do. He stood there paralysed as the darkness came closer. It was moving rapidly. As it got to his street, it swallowed the houses, trees, lamp posts, cars and birds. Everything it touched was swallowed into nothing. Their existence was being erased in front of Dylan's eyes. *His* own reality. It was over. The Deadly Dimension caught up with the cement people and they were soon gone. And then, before he knew it, the whole street that he lived on wasn't there. There wasn't anything at all. Nothing existed any more. The Deadly Dimension had swallowed everything. Except for Mr Ebenezer's shop. And that meant, maybe not quite everything had gone. There must still be some hope. There was still someone left from RTH-0709 thought Dylan.

'I'm still here... I'm still here!' He said out loud.

'So I can see, Master Thompson,' came a familiar voice from behind.

13

MR EBENEZER WAS standing in front of the desk with his hands on his hips.

'Mr Ebenezer...'

'Yes? You are an inconvenience you know, young man. I am terribly busy. Would you mind running along so that I can carry on with my work?'

'I can't *run along*. Have you seen outside? There isn't one. It's gone. It's all gone, erased from existence by the Deadly Dimension.'

Mr Ebenezer glanced out of the window casually.

'Oh, so it has. Now that is a shame. Well, I don't know what you were expecting, but you can't stay here.'

Dylan looked to where the door from his house had been. It was no longer there. His only choice was to stay in this shop. Or investigate what was in that dark corner.

'So you know what the Deadly Dimension is?' he asked Mr Ebenezer.

'*Do I know what the Deadly Dimension is...* have you been attending school, Thompson? Of course I know.'

'And so you know that there are other realities?'

Mr Ebenezer snorted derisively, but didn't say anything.

'Well, if the Deadly Dimension eats all reality into nothingness, how come your shop is still here? How come *we're* still here? It's right outside the shop, so how come everything is the same as usual in here?'

'Questions, questions! We are still here, because I have been *sensible*! It was almost ruined by you and your friend when you knocked the books all over the place, but luckily I got them all back into position in time.'

'The *books*?'

'Yes, the books! Why else do you think I arranged them like that? Not exactly conducive to selling them. Their exact arrangement is what is protecting this shop.'

Dylan thought this over.

'So you knew about this was all going to happen. If you were preparing to defend yourself against it, but not warn anyone else... did *you* create the Deadly Dimension?'

Mr Ebenezer threw his arms up in anger.

'Did I create it? No I did not! I tried to prevent it. I *had* been hoping that you and your friend Rollo would work out how to do so. But it soon became apparent that wouldn't happen too soon...'

'How did you know about Rollo? Who *are* you?'

'That's none of your business. Oh, I wish you had stayed down that well. Such a nuisance.'

'You were trying to get rid of us!'

Mr Ebenezer laughed.

'Of course!' He started walking towards Dylan. 'And it really *is* time you left now.'

'But, the Deadly Dimension,' said Dylan. 'I can help you get rid of it. Rollo told me something just before he was got,' he lied. 'Please.'

'I'm not going to get rid of it. I've changed my mind about getting rid of it. I'm going to create everything again. From scratch. The way that *I* want it.'

Mr Ebenezer dived to grab hold of Dylan, but he was too quick and ducked under his arm, and ran to the passageway between the books. He ran far in among them, twisting around the corridors created by the stacks. He looked behind him quickly. Mr Ebenezer wasn't there.

'I know where you are, Master Thompson. There's nowhere to go. You know that. In fact, it's *nowhere* that I want you to go.'

Dylan crept further along into the books. He looked up towards the dark corner of the room. Going into that corner, whatever lay beyond it was his only chance. He couldn't leave the shop any other way, and he couldn't stay there with Mr Ebenezer.

He listened for any signs of movement. He could hear footsteps creeping along, getting closer. He started moving again, quietly but with more haste. He had turned where two paths between the books met, thinking he would be closer to the dark corner, but it took him further away.

He retraced his steps. He wasn't sure which way he had come from. He started down one path but found himself at a dead end and had to go back.

When he returned to the cross road, there was something waiting for him. It was the snake again. 'Just what I need,' thought Dylan as he froze in his tracks. The snake didn't move, or make any threatening gestures. It was looking at him with big eyes, its head raised. Slowly, it turned away and began slithering away from him. After a few metres it stopped and looked back at him expectantly. Dylan shrugged his shoulders. It was more likely the snake knew where it was going than he did. He followed it and the snake slithered onward, checking every now and then to make sure that Dylan was still following. As they twisted and turned between the books, they were soon at their destination.

Books were stacked a metre and a half in front of the corner. The snake slithered between the gaps of two of the books and was gone. Dylan heard footsteps behind him. He spun round.

'Oh, so that's your escape plan is it? Through the hole I made into that irritating, what did they call it... sanctuary. It's no use. You can't get through it. Not if I can't. Believe me.'

'No,' said Dylan, 'I won't believe you.'

He pushed over the books blocking his way.

'Not the books, you fool!' screamed Mr Ebenezer.

Dylan tried to jump over the fallen books, but Mr Ebenezer managed to leap forward and just caught Dylan by the ankle so that he fell over. Dylan could see that the ceiling was being rolled back and that the Deadly Dimension, that solid darkness was coming towards them, fast. Mr Ebenezer hadn't noticed. He was too intent on trying to pull Dylan towards him. He struggled, but Mr Ebenezer's grip was too strong. Dylan looked in terror as the Deadly Dimension raced towards them. Suddenly, Mr Ebenezer saw the look of horror on his face. He turned his head and cried out in fear, letting go of Dylan as the Deadly Dimension caught up with them and started erasing Mr Ebenezer's legs. Dylan sprang up and sprinted into the corner —not a moment too soon.

14

THERE WAS DARKNESS there, too, but of a different kind. It didn't feel solid, horrible or hostile. He ran as deep into it as he could, then he stopped, panted, trying to regain his breath. He looked behind him, but there was only darkness. But it wasn't the Deadly Dimension. As far as he was aware, he wouldn't exist anymore if the Deadly Dimension had caught up with him, and he was still in existence. He was still thinking, certainly still breathing. Up ahead, in the distance, there was some light. When he had caught his breath, he started walking forwards again.

He kept an ear out for anything behind him, but there was nothing but silence. At first it had been impossible to tell what kind of place he was in. The ground had been hard and level. As he went along, the air became cooler and a breeze came from the direction of the light. He put his arms out to his sides to see if he could feel walls, but there was nothing close by. He knelt and touched the ground. It was cold and felt like stone. A drip of water landed on his face. He was in a cave, he guessed. He wondered what would be outside it, whether it was the closed sanctuary Mr Ebenezer had mentioned. Rollo had said that sanctuaries were dark and empty, unless there was someone inside who had a powerful enough imagination. Judging by the light ahead, whoever had sealed himself in the sanctuary had just that. Dylan wondered what it would be like. He wondered who he was. Rollo had said to the Intrapelatio Council that this person had created the Deadly Dimension. Dylan's heart sank. He was on his own now. There was no Rollo or Audrey to help him, and his father and everyone else no longer existed. It was just him. There was no choice but to confront this person or creature and see if there was any way to put things right again. Until he knew otherwise, he was going to continue trying to believe it was possible. It would be too painful to contemplate otherwise. Eventually, Dylan reached the end of the darkness and stumbled into the light. He seemed to be emerging from a cave. He blinked, shielding his eyes at the sudden brightness.

His eyes quickly grew accustomed to the light. The sky was blue with white clouds drifting around in it. The clouds were shaped like faces with some crude detail. They had eyes he was sure were actually moving around, and mouths that occasionally turned into creepy smiles.

Around him was luscious green grass amongst rocks and trees, all twisted like the bonsai trees that his grandfather grew. He looked behind him to where he had come from. Where the mouth of the cave had been was now just stone. The bottom of a mountain that stretched high up into the sky.

In front of him was a hill. On its peak, under the shade of a tree, a llama stood, staring down at him and munching on something. Dylan couldn't see a sun in the sky, but he felt a warm gentle breeze. The place had a happy feel that made everything that had happened seemed remote. He heard a cry of a seagull wheeling above him in the air. It was a little larger than any seagulls he had seen before, and purple. Maybe there was a sea. He had a strong yearning to see it, if there was.

He started up the hill towards the llama. There would be a good view from up there. He climbed the hill slowly. It was such a nice day. He hummed to himself as he went. A while later he reached the top. He wondered how long it had taken. He looked at his wristwatch, but the LCD screen was blank. He walked over to the llama that was still watching him, munching away on something. Bits of book pages were sticking out of its mouth. It was probably the one he had seen in Mr Ebenezer's bookshop before.

'Hello. Can you talk?' he asked.

The llama shook its head.

'You didn't create the Deadly Dimension did you?'

Again the llama shook its head.

'Have you seen anyone else around?'

The llama nodded, tilting its head towards a long grassy valley below, speckled with a strange variety of strongly coloured plants and trees, he had never seen. Beyond the valley, were high cliffs crowned by a building of white stone topped by high twisted spires. In the distance, a huge ocean spread out in front of him. The water was sometimes blue, sometimes purple, sometimes green and sometimes yellow. He couldn't see anyone.

'Is there someone in that building on the cliff?'

The llama shook its head.

As he made his way down the hill, a salty sea breeze reached his nostrils. More purple seagulls cried out above the sea, circling and diving for fish. One flew out above him, crying again and again. He could have sworn it was saying *chips, chips, chips, chips*. He walked out across the sand to the edge of the water. The water was remarkably calm, despite the breeze. He found a flat stone and skimmed it. Usually he only managing two or three bounces, but this one went on and on, disappearing into the distance.

Whoever had created the Deadly Dimension must be up in that building crowning the cliff, but as he approached the building seemed to melt away. In its place was an oval white stone, about fifty metres high. Whoever had created the Deadly Dimension must be changing things to trick him and was likely to be where most changes occurred.

Suddenly the sea let out a loud roar, the water rose as if it was going to become a giant tidal wave, but instead of crashing forward, the entire sea rose into the air, revealing damp sand below. As it rose, the water turned into a canopy of green leaves floating trunkless in the air. The sand in front of him, covered by water only moments before, stirred and rose, turning into the figure of a man, towering above him like the mast of a ship. Dylan shivered. It reminded him of the cement people that had got Audrey and Rollo.

He stood still, eyes fixed on the huge figure. He had nowhere to run to. He was inside a sanctuary and that meant that he might be *inside* the imagination of the very person he was trying to escape! The sand figure was a lot less rough and ready than the cement people. It stood above Dylan angling its featureless face down towards him. It was about five times the size of a normal human.

'You, strange little *being*,' it boomed. 'Who *are* you?'

'I was going to ask you the same question,' Dylan replied.

'It does not matter who *I* am. *You* are the one that doesn't belong here.'

'You don't belong here either, from what I've heard. Didn't you lock yourself in the sanctuary illegally? And create the Deadly Dimension— which would make you a mass murderer too.'

The sand man swooped down a hand, grabbed Dylan and lifted him up so that he was level with its face. A he did so, he grew larger still, breaking through the canopy of leaves.

'MURDERER?' He shouted.

Wind whipped at Dylan's face. He had to shout to be heard.

'Yes. You stopped everything from existing. Not just people. All things. You're even worse than a murderer.'

The sandy hand gripped Dylan tighter and it began to hurt.

'Who are you?' he asked again.

Dylan struggled to get more room to breathe.

'I'm just a boy. I'm just a human boy.'

'A human? I know of these humans. How did you get into the sanctuary?'

'I came in through...through a dark corner. That's what it looked like in my world, a dark corner. I wandered through that darkness into a cave and into here.'

'A dark corner? There is only one way into the sanctuary and it is not from your world. But there *has* been a leak. Where *was* this corner?'

'In... in Mr Ebenezer's shop!'

'EBENEZER?'

The sand man turned Dylan upside down, bringing his face close to Dylan's.

'YOU WORK FOR EBENEZER?'

Dylan was almost deafened. The blood rushed to his head. He tried not to think about how far he might fall, if he was dropped.

'**ANSWER ME!**'

'No!' shouted Dylan.

The sand man paused for a few moments.

'So the leak was Ebenezer trying to get in? I thought as much. If the way you came in was through his 'shop', what were you doing coming through it, if you are not working for him?'

'I was trying to get *away* from him.'

The sand man looked puzzled.

'I wanted to find whoever created the Deadly Dimension.'

Silence.

'Could you turn me the right way up now? It's hard to talk like this.'

The sand man turned Dylan back the right way. He shrank to the size that he had been before. He strode across the land towards the cliff-top. He was holding his hand out straight now so that Dylan could sit on it. Dylan peered over the edge. He hoped the sand man wasn't going to decide to get rid of him too soon. It would only need to turn its hand over and Dylan would go tumbling towards his death.

With long strides the sand man climbed the cliffs. He walked to the spot where the huge white oval stone was.

Slowly, he lowered his hand and put Dylan next to the oval stone. He looked up at him, the sand man was crumbling, his huge body turning into a pile of sand.

'There must be someone else here,' Dylan said out loud. 'That can't have been the guy the llama wanted me to meet. That llama knew something. He must have meant someone else.'

'I guess that would be me,' came a voice from behind him.

Dylan froze. He knew the sound of that voice.

'Rollo!'

He turned round and there he was! Rollo was leaning against the bottom of the oval stone wearing his rain coat and bowler hat, looking just like he had when he first met him.

'Rollo! I can't believe it! Where's Audrey, did she make it too?'

'Audrey? I don't know anyone by the name of Audrey. And it's Rollovkarghjicznilegogh-Vylpophyngh, thank you very much.'

'Rollo, it's me Dylan.'

Rollo looked at him carefully.

'I don't know any Dylans. And I never had so much as a chance to talk to a human being. Unless you count Ebenezer. But I don't think you can.'

'You don't remember me?'

Rollo looked at him quizzically. 'You human beings

don't seem to be the brightest. No, young man. This is the first time I've seen you.'

Rollo must somehow have survived the Deadly Dimension and ended up here but lost his memory. Or perhaps this wasn't Rollo at all, but someone else disguised as Rollo. Or—and that was an awesome possibility—perhaps Rollo or some part of Rollo or his twin had been in the sanctuary all along and had created the Deadly Dimension. His head was spinning with all the different possibilities.

'You were trying to get away from Ebenezer? I can see he didn't get in here with you. All hell would have broken loose if he had. What happened to you before you got here?'

'Everything went weird in my reality. There was not just the Deadly Dimension. There were all these holes to other dimensions, other realities. And then all the normal people, human beings, had vanished and there were these cement people chasing us.'

'Oh, that was me! I'm sorry if they frightened you. You see, I found there was a leak in the sanctuary when the llama kept wandering off and coming back munching book pages. I guessed it was Ebenezer trying to get in, so I put let my imagination run riot in order to try and stop him—I sent my imaginary beings through that dark corner in his shop. Cement men, I thought, I'll attack him with cement men.'

'Well, that didn't stop him. In fact, they nearly stopped me, and they did get my friend Audrey. And they got *you*.'

'Did they? Oops... It was a bit of a gamble,' said Rollo calmly. 'But Ebenezer, what happened to him?'

'The Deadly Dimension caught up with him just before I got through to here.'

Rollo clapped his hands together.

'Excellent! That's one thing that's gone right.'

'But aren't you worried that the cement people turned you into one of them...'

Rollo looked at him. His featureless egg face was giving nothing away.

'Hmm...I wasn't planning on that. But I'm still here. I trust myself. I *did* have a plan for all of this.'

'Please tell me,' shouted Dylan. 'Are you Rollo, *my* Rollo?'

'I think so,' he said thoughtfully, continuing after a long silence. 'Something really weird happened to me, or I should say to happened to *us* when we were both *me*. I'm kind of the guy you met.' Another silence and then Rollo's familiar voice. His way of talking too, a bit formal. 'I had been on an assignment for the IU, tracking Ebenezer. Did the Rollo you met tell you that there were other realities? I can't imagine it was common knowledge in RTH-0709 just yet.'

Dylan shook his head. 'You were tracking Mr Ebenezer? Is he from my reality?'

'No—well I don't know exactly. I have theories. I haven't found much on his background and it's not clear what or who he is. He does look like one of you, human beings, but as he seems very good at traveling to different realities and RTH-0709 was very much untapped until now, it's unlikely. But he and his *shop*, as you called it, have been turning up in numerous places. He's been stealing books, stealing fiction from all different realities. After some research it became clear that whatever he is, he's been into the IU's classified files. I only gained access to them because it was relevant to my assignment. There is a case from a few millennia ago concerning a *kirikiriki* being named Trkaka who was devising a way of control-ling and shaping whole realities through collecting certain books and arranging them in a secret order. He had a brilliant idea and he got very close to to making it work. He took thousands of books from the reality or realities to be controlled. Then put them together to create a completely new book. Something that's never existed before. The Final Book. With the Final Book you can control everything. It seems that Ebenezer worked out what Trkaka never did. Although it is down to *one person* to gather and arrange the texts, the Final Book with its special powers will not exist until someone else, someone *completely separate* gives it a name.'

Dylan looked at him thunderstruck.

'Oh, my God!'

'I learnt this through spying on Ebenezer.' continued Rollo. 'When he realised I knew what he was up to, he went on the run, flitting between realities like nobody's business. He thought he could shake me off easily, but he didn't know that I'm the best tracker in the IU. And it was fine, I kept following him wherever he went, and there were no problems until I followed him to RTH-0709, your reality. As it was untapped, I couldn't slip there at all easily. I found myself caught between realities and the only thing I could do was to try and slip into RTH-0709 in Ebenezer's wake. I was only partially successful. The part of me you met managed to get through just fine, but the slipping cut us in two. One half of me slipped away, while I was left between realities— and that isn't safe. I panicked and slipped to the first place I knew I would have some safety — here. I'm not authorised to ever have been in here, but I've never found it easy to play within the rules. That's when I came up with a plan, and locked myself in here.'

'And... you created the Deadly Dimension?!'

'Of course I did!'

'WHAT KIND OF PLAN IS THAT?' shouted Dylan. He was furious.

'A very good one, I think you'll find.'

'The Deadly Dimension has been erasing all realities out of existence. Mine is gone! All of it. Everything and everyone I have ever known is gone. And it's *your* fault.

How is eradicating everything going to help? What *was* the plan?'

'Hmm… That's the thing,' said Rollo, not at all flummoxed by Dylan's anger. 'I can't quite remember.'

'You don't remember?' Dylan stared at him in amazement.

'I know that I made the Deadly Dimension. I created it in here with my imagination and let it loose in between realities to find its own way, so that it would erase everything in existence, including Ebenezer and his books, stopping him from gaining control of everything with all the fantasy of fiction he'd been collecting. Somehow, I was going bring everything back again after it was all destroyed.'

'How would you bring everything back again?'

'Goodness knows. I know it was an excellent plan, but I've forgotten the second half of it where everything gets put right. I think that when I split in two, the half you knew took most of the capacity for creating new memories. I'm so forgetful, you can't believe it.'

'So there's no hope.'

'Oh, there's hope. There's always hope, as long as you still exist… Ah, there you are.'

Something was slithering towards them—the snake, the very one that Dylan had seen down the plughole! It seemed so long ago. Rollo picked it up and it coiled around his neck and flicked its tongue at Dylan.

'Is that your snake?'

'My pet. I was a bit lonely, so I imagined some animals to keep me company. Everything in the sanctuary is made from my imagination. That sand man was controlled by me. I don't know where the ideas came from, but I made them up.'

'The snake and the llama? And the purple seagulls?'

Rollo nodded. 'How do you know their names when I created them?'

'You didn't make them up. They're from my world—although seagulls aren't purple.'

'Hmm...,' he scratched his head. 'There's a good chance there's a telepathic link between me and the other Rollo, what with us being the same person. Maybe he saw them in your reality.'

'That snake! I've seen it a few times. In my bathroom at home. And it tried attacking me and Audrey in the bookshop.'

'Oh, you can't be too hard on it. It was making sure that nothing got in here. Not sure how it ended up in your bathroom though.'

At that moment there was a boom somewhere in the sanctuary.

'What was that?'

'Good question.'

The noise had come from far above the canopy of green, which suddenly turned back into water, crashing onto to the sand below and becoming an ocean once again.

'I didn't do that!' shouted Rollo. 'Someone else is in here.'

'It isn't the Deadly Dimension?'

'No. It can't enter the sanctuary. And it wouldn't undo my imaginings like it just did. It's a person. And whoever it is has got as powerful an imagination as I have.'

There was something in the sky. It looked like a huge dragonfly with something hanging from where its mouth must be, something dangling at the end of a rope.

'There!' Dylan pointed.

'Aha, let's see if we can capture them.'

Rollo put his hand to his forehead. The water below the dragonfly rose in a pillar heading for it, collapsing before it reached it and tumbling back where it had come from, doing no harm.

'Must try harder.'

The dragonfly was making quick progress, but it was still too far away to see what or who was dangling at the end of the rope. As it flew, the outline of a box appeared around it, fading in and out.

'Ha, he or she is trying to stop me. No chance.'

The box became solid metal, a dull iron colour. It floated through the air.

'Got them! Let's bring them over here.'

The box started moving towards them.

'Do you think it's safe?'

'Don't talk. Whoever is in there is trying their best to get out.'

'Trying? I'm already out.'

They looked up. The box had opened. The dragonfly was hovering above them, and dangling down from its mouth, at the end of a rope, was a being without a face. Rollo—Dylan's Rollo!

15

'DYLAN! You made it! Very well done, young bean.'
Rollo clapped Dylan on the shoulder.

Dylan was pleased to see the Rollo he knew, but he wasn't going to show it. He had too many important questions.

'Where's Audrey? How did you survive? And where is she?'

Rollo hesitated for the first time since Dylan had known him. He bowed his head a little.

'I couldn't save her, Dylan.'

'What? Rollo, you just left her?'

'No more than you did. When the cement people got us, the only option I had was to slip. The cement covered me too fast for me to be able to save her. Look here I am, no clothes just underpants.'

The two jelli creatures were standing in front of him, identical except one was wearing a rain coat and bowler hat and the other was only in underpants. The two Rollos looked too pleased with themselves. Dylan wondered whether either of them cared at all for what happened to anyone else or the world or any of the many realities. It all seemed like one big joke to to them.

'You *do* know that it was you, you or your second self that created the Deadly Dimension?'

'Dylan...' Rollo didn't say anything for a few moments. 'Yes, I did have my suspicions.'

'Suspicions?'

'OK, I...I was 99% sure that it was me in the sanctuary, *and* that I'd created the Deadly Dimension.'

'And you didn't say anything! You knew all along, right from when I first met you. *You* were the cause of the problems all along!'

'Dylan, I couldn't risk letting anyone know that I suspected that *I* had locked myself in the sanctuary or that I had created the Deadly Dimension. If the IU had gotten wind of that, they would lock me away in a slarpup prison. That or a secure mental health clinic. No one would believe me if I started telling them that I had split in two. There's only one recorded instance of that happening, and that was over a thousand years ago.'

Dylan sighed. 'How did you even get in here? I thought you couldn't slip into a sanctuary?'

'Not usually. Because you can't visualise what's inside, and there's nothing to guide you. But you helped with that. Remember that tracking device I gave you to throw into that dark hole?' Rollo pulled a shiny black square object out of a pocket and pressed something on it.

A beeping noise came from the other Rollo's pocket. He pulled out the tracking device that Dylan had thrown into the dark corner in Mr Ebenezer's shop.

'The llama found this. I couldn't quite remember if I had imagined it into existence or not.'

'Couldn't quite remember,' thought Dylan. 'Or didn't really care.' He looked at their featureless faces. They were really giving him the creeps.

'I'm pretty sure I know what your plan was,' said Rollo in underpants to Rollo in bowler hat.

'Excellent! Because I've completely forgotten. I remember thinking that creating the Deadly Dimension was a marvellous idea, and then the rest of the plan seemed to blow away on the breeze…'

'It's quite simple. Creating the Deadly Dimension would obviously obliterate everything, hopefully including Mr Ebenezer, and his books. But first, you would have to obtain the Final Book.'

'Aha! Yes, that's it! I remember. The Final Book! It makes sense now. Where is it?'

'What!' Rollo threw his hands in the air. 'I don't have it. I thought *you* would have it. You were making the hole from here into Ebenezer's shop to get it.'

'The leak? *That* was Ebenezer trying to get in here. Seeming as you were footloose and fancy free on the outside, I thought that once you had worked out the plan, you would have got the book and found a way of bringing it here.'

All three looked at each other. Suddenly Dylan felt an overwhelming urge to laugh—it was all just too terrible.

'So you've destroyed the world and let loose the Deadly Dimension by mistake!'

'Don't make fun of us, Dylan,' said Rollo. 'It's not the right time. We've messed up our plan and destroyed all reality in the process. It'll just be the sanctuaries left when the Deadly Dimension is through.'

'*Unusual Land Animals of No Small Consequence!*'

'What's he on about?' asked the Rollo in the bowler hat. The other Rollo shrugged his shoulders.

'You know what you said about the Final Book, how it would only be created when someone, an outsider named it?'

They both nodded

'That was *me*. I gave the Final Book its name. The first time I met Mr Ebenezer in his bookshop he asked me what I was looked for. He was weirding me out, so I just made up the title. *Unusual Land Animals of No Small Consequence*. I made it up, but then it was in his catalogue.'

'Ha! That must be it!' Rollo clapped his hands together. 'But it's not much use if we don't have it,' he said slowly with infuriating obviousness.

Dylan felt his pocket. He had completely forgotten. He had found it in the bookshop just before they had been chased out by the snake. That's why the snake had clamped his jaws around the book. He had put it in his pocket at the tube station to look at later but he had never had the time, too much had been going on. He pulled it out.

'Here it is!'

'Dylan! You're amazing!' said Rollo.

'Splendiferous!' said the second Rollo.

'A hero!' They both linked arms and danced a jig in a circle.

Dylan laughed. He couldn't stop laughing. 'Does this mean that we can put things right? Bring back everything the Deadly Dimension erased?'

'The Final Book contains all the information about everything in every universe in every reality. It's all in here. Every little bit. All we need to do is slip in between realities and imagine the book bringing everything back. The book will explode in a big bang, turning into the realities. That's the theory anyway.'

'You risked *all* realities on a theory?'

'It was that or risk Ebenezer taking control of all realities. You have to gamble sometimes,' said bowler hat Rollo.

'But...but ... if you bring everything back, won't Mr Ebenezer come back too? And all his books? Is there any way to get rid of him?'

'It would be very complicated to do. Possible.'

'Then shouldn't we try to do it?' asked Dylan.

'We could. But it's not really our right to permanently

erase someone from existence. He should be given fair trial, like anyone else.'

'What's to stop him just carrying on as he was when we take everything back to how it was?'

'That won't happen. The Final Book won't exist anymore. The rest of the books are the only things we'll interfere with. We'll imagine that they're all back in their own realities and in the correct places. The IU have put ultra-high security in place on their original locations. Mr Ebenezer would have to do something very impressive to get them back into his hands.'

Silence. A thought suddenly struck Dylan.

'And what will happen to him?'

'He'll go on the run. He might leave your reality, or he might hide in it. I doubt that he will, but keep your eyes peeled. We will hopefully become one again when we slip. I hope so anyway. Although it could be useful being split in two in our line of work.'

'Ready?'

One of them took the book. They were standing on either side of Dylan, each with a hand on his shoulder.

'I'll miss having my own little world,' said the second Rollo looking over the sea and land he had created. 'Time to go,' said the other. 'Time to dance between realities. Hold on and imagine...'

The three of them slipped. Everything around him went dark.

16

DYLAN WAS IN darkness. There was no one else. Nothing at all. He just floated, unable to feel his body or breath. It was neither warm nor cold. It wasn't any different from the other times he had slipped, but it was lasting a lot longer. He felt panicky. The two Rollos' plan had better work. He didn't want to be trapped in an abyss of darkness forever—worse than being swallowed by the Deadly Dimension. He called out to hear his own voice, but nothing came out. After what seemed like forever, there was a sudden burst of colour far away, in front of him. It came rushing towards him, pulling at his being. He felt air blowing straight past him and heard a strange pop. Air filled his lungs. His eyes were dazzled by electric light.

First he couldn't see anything, then his eyes got accustomed to the brightness. He looked about himself. He was in his bedroom. The curtains were drawn, but through a crack he could see that it was dark outside. There was another pop and Rollo was standing in front of him. Just one Rollo.

'Haha!' he shouted. 'We did it!' He high-fived Dylan. 'Excellent work, Dylan! Bloody good job you had that book!'

'You're one again!' said Dylan. 'Unless you lost the other bit of you?'

Rollo looked himself over and patted himself. 'Pretty sure I'm all in the one body again!'

'So, is everything back the way it should be?'

'Oh yes, not a thing out of place. Though I do think that if you take a visit to a certain bookshop, you will find a closed sign on the door. There shouldn't be any dodgy cross-reality confusions anymore either, you'll be glad to hear.'

'Amazing. What happens now?'

'Well, I'm going to return to my own reality to have a nap. Then I suppose I ought to report back to the IU. Then I'll be back on the hunt after Mr Ebenezer, make sure he doesn't get up to any more mischief.'

Dylan was quiet.

'What's up?'

'I know the whole time things have been happening, I wanted everything to go back to normal,' said Dylan slowly. 'But it was exciting. Things *were* happening. And now you're going to go away and life is going to go back to being boring.'

'Ho!' said Rollo. 'Nonsense. Life is never boring. And you never know what's coming around the corner. Keep your eyes and your ears open, Dylan. If you don't like what you see, make it better. There's always a way to do so.'

'I guess.'

'No guessing about it, dear boy. Now, time for me to be off.'

'Will... will I see you again?' asked Dylan.

'I can't say for certain, old chap. RTH-0709 is still classified information. If the IU do decide to make contact and enlighten those of your reality to everything else out there, it will only be after many years' research. And they might decide to delay doing so until your people have made certain advances, or that RTH-0709 is best left in the dark about the presence of other realities. Technically I won't be allowed back in the meantime unless it relates to an assignment. But we'll see. You may have noticed that I don't always fit in with the IU's rules and regulations.'

If Rollo had eyes, he would have winked.

'Well, I'll miss you Rollo.'

'You too, young Dylan, you too. It has been a pleasure to know you. Hang on.'

Rollo pulled something out of his pocket and threw it to Dylan. Dylan caught it. It was the tracking device.

'If you are ever really in a jam, give, that a good firm squeeze,' Rollo said. He lifted a finger. 'And if you are ever tempted to try slipping on your own again, please don't. It's too dangerous without the proper training.

Only do it if you're really, really stuck, and you've lost that tracking device.'

Dylan nodded.

'Goodbye, young Dylan. It's been a pleasure.'

'It's been great. Goodbye Rollo.'

Rollo did a funny salute and with another pop it was like he had never been there at all.

Dylan sat on his bed and looked down at the tracking device in his hand.

His mobile phone beeped. He picked it up. It was a text message from Audrey.

Dylan!!! What's going on?? One minute the cement people had us—the next I'm standing there in the dark and you and Rollo weren't there. And everything is back like normal. I'm on a bus back home. Are you OK? Is everything fixed? Let me know you're OK. If you are, you're going to tell me EVERY-THING tomorrow! My head is so messed up.

Dylan laughed. He texted back.

Yep. All normal. Long story! Will tell you everything tomorrow.

There was a knock on his door. He quickly stuffed the tracking device in his pocket. His dad popped his head around the door with a concerned look on his face.

'Is everything alright, Dylan?' he asked. 'I heard a shout a few minutes ago and it sounded like you were talking to yourself.'

Laughing Dylan jumped up and hugged his dad.

'I'm fine, Dad. Everything is great.'

His dad smiled.

'I'm very pleased to hear that. Very pleased. I was coming to see if you want to come down for our comedy? It's on in a minute.'

'I'd love to,' said Dylan. 'I just need to go to the loo first.'

Dylan went to the bathroom. He pulled the light cord and went over to the sink. He took a deep breath, leaned over and looked down the plughole. It was just an ordinary plughole. So that's the end of all the weirdness, he thought. He could feel the transmitter through the outside of his pocket. For now, anyway.

About the author

Mark Bardwell grew up in Croydon and currently lives in London, following excursions to Bangor University and to the fine city of Norwich. He is a voracious reader of books, and is happiest when writing stories, listening to live music, exploring the countryside, contemplating the universe and eating peanut butter on crumpets. Dylan and the Deadly Dimension is his first book for children.